Ballad of
Forgotten Years

Ballad of Forgotten Years

Abish Kekilbayev

Introduced by Tom Stacey

STACEY
INTERNATIONAL

Ballad of Forgotten Years

Published by
Stacey International
128 Kensington Church Street
London W8 4BH
Telephone: +44 (0)20 7221 7166 Fax: +44 (0)20 7792 9288
E-mail: info@stacey-international.co.uk
www.stacey-international.co.uk

ISBN: 978-1-905299-66-9

© Abish Kekilbayev and Stacey International 2008

Draft translation (from the Russian) by Samantha Kolupov

The right of Abish Kekilbayev to be identified as the author of this work
has been asserted by him in accordance with the Copyright, Designs
and Patents Act of 1988.

CIP Data: A catalogue record for this book is available from the British Library

Printed in Dubai by Oriental Press

All rights reserved. No part of this publication may be reproduced, stored
in a retrieval system, or transmitted in any form or by any means, electronic,
mechanical, photocopying, recording, or otherwise, without the prior
permission of the copyright owners.

Introduction

The *Ballad of Forgotten Years* is a rare, not to say eccentric, piece of contemporary fiction. There will be assuredly nothing quite like it available elsewhere to the English-speaking reader. Conceived in the Kazakh idiom by the old man of strictly Kazakh letters, Abish Kekilbayev (born in 1939), and set down originally in that language, it has come to us in this English rendering by way of the Russian language edition of 2003.

The *Ballad* draws with devout precision – at times disquietingly so – upon the realities of tribal life and its unrelenting feuds on the central Asian steppe of a 'forgotten' past, at a point in social history which is wilfully undefined yet which plausibly belongs to a period before the entry of firearms in the early eighteenth century but after the spread of Islam across the steppe in the twelfth century. The narrative before us places the rival semi-nomadic tribal groups involved, the Turkmen and the Kazakhs, living and grazing their flocks and horses in loose juxtaposition, in Mangistau, at a point not far from the shores of a 'sea' which can only be one of the two great expanses of inland salt water of today's eastern Kazakhstan, the Aral and the Caspian.

Let us not strain for exactitude. For this is a ballad, half-myth, in the bardic tradition of mediaeval man, a tradition reaching from Hunnic China to Celtic Britain. The cultural taproot of this short, egregious work is therefore oral and musical; and music, in the tale itself, is the implied redemptive element. The Kazakh language today in central Asia bears to Russian something of the relationship of Welsh to English in our own Britain, albeit across a vastly greater region. Of today's Kazakhstan, the ninth largest country in the world, somewhat more than half its native population of fourteen or so million are of Kazakh blood, among whom – notwithstanding some two centuries of Russian and Russifying colonisation, ruthless throughout the mid-twentieth century and coming close to a total ethnic cleansing – the Kazakh language just held on. Something of the suffering of the *mankurti* we read of here may be said to have been undergone by the remnant Kazakh survivors of the 20th century ordeal – in each case those who through the intensity of their suffering lose awareness of who they truly are and what their inheritance has been. Yet here we are in the 21st century, and the Kazakh tongue and its literary tradition are experiencing a revival.

The mantle of the towering figure of nineteenth-century Kazakh letters, Abai Kunanbayev (1845-1904), falls across Kekilbayev's shoulders: Abai the poet, romancer, balladist, sage and, indeed – like

Kekilbayev – public figure and administrator. Both in their way have drawn creatively on a vein of poetic and bardic utterance with mingled Farsi, Arabic and Turkic sources, and thus shared by Firdausi, Hafez, Saadi, Sakhali and others. The prose of Kekilbayev's *Ballad* comes across awkwardly to contemporary English ears, as awkwardly and oddly as a Welsh ballad reaches us, with the rightful harp accompaniment out of earshot and the crackling logs in the hearth out of view, and with image and adjectival multiplicity heaped on one another in mounting configurations of speech known to the scholar of mediaeval Welsh as *dyfal*. By a comparable linguistic token, the narratives of the ballads of each are soaked in the landscape and its inherent human-and-animal drama: what the *mynnydd-dir*, the mountain-land, is to the bardic Welsh, so is the steppe to the bardic Kazakh and its literary exponents, as far as the present-day voice of Abish Kekilbayev.

Islam began to penetrate the vast half-empty steppe some eight hundred years ago from northern Persia and the Caspian across to the Altai and Tien Shan mountain ranges of western China. It entered a scattered, pastoral, transhumant community in their ever-exposed *auls* and yurts, enduring a ferocious annual climatic cycle, in primal fear of rivalry for pasture. The new religion brought a welcome discipline and structure, however vestigial, among a people which hitherto belonged to an indigenous shamanism bearing the further spiritual influence of Nestorian Christianity from the West and Zoroastrianism from the South. The new faith thus primarily took up its mystic, Sufic form, offsetting and somehow alleviating the savagery which sheer survival on the steppe seemed to entail. In all this, the soul's balm was ever music and the musician's inspired improvisation on the Kazakh steppe's stringed instruments, the *dombra* and the *dutar*.

It is related to this day how, when the pagan Genghiz swept from his Mongolian heartland in the far north-east (with the embryonic Kazakh race part of his confederal horde), across that steppe and thereafter half the world, that which alone tamed his rampaging breast and filled his eyes with tears was the sound of the *dombra* of the Kazakh Jeti-Su. The modern mind is dizzied by such polarity. This same secret, tenuous sound the reader may hear anew in what Kekilbayev recovers from his own folk-memory in his *Ballad of Forgotten Years*. Listen for it, and be dizzied.

Tom Stacey
London, May 2008

Chapter I

On a broad knoll, burned by the sun's midday heat, in the rays of a tremulous haze, there stands a Turkmen village, an *aul*, which looks as if it is floating on the endless sea of the steppe. Take a look out and you will see how bare the steppe is, without so much as a hill to be seen – only the flat plain cracked open by the intense heat. And only on the far side of the *aul*, on the hazy horizon, will you see an isolated burial mound jutting against the skyline like the tip of a spear. On the summit of the burial mound you will see a watchman surveying far-off enemy lands. At the back of the watchman, from the *aul,* itself, a pair of deep-set beady eyes gleam from under the thrown-back opening of the yurt.

From the high point of the sentry's terracotta knoll, with sides so steep one would think them man-made, the views of the steppe reach far and wide, and the Turkmen villagers sit and survey the surrounding distances. Well may they be content, in the midday languor under the fierce heat of the sun, to breathe in the familiar scents of steppe life at peace: the astringent odours of horse urine and human sweat, the fragrance of steppe herbs. All is quiet, sleepy and intensely hot. Even the gangling young camels have ceased their gambolling among the yurt dwellings, but instead are lying down behind the yurts in the shade. Inside the yurts themselves everything has stopped and gone quiet. The Turkmen in their shabby *papakhas*, their tall hats of sheepskin, sit in a circle against the walls, in silence, no longer exchanging glances. Some have half-shut their eyes, their heads slumping onto their chests, making a pecking movement with predatory noses as they doze off. Even the tea in the bulbous, stripy urn has been left untouched.

The silhouette of the watchman stands out on the top of the mound erect and motionless like a driven-in stake. But now all the heads in the tall *papakhas* have one by one drooped onto their chests, as if unable to sustain the weight of the fur hats. Just one of those in the yurt – a swarthy man with a harsh, crinkled face and a greying forked beard stands unmoving, his shoulders squared and barrel chest thrust out. With those deep-set eyes he continues to scrutinise the watchman on the top of the far-off mound. His bushy eyebrows look as if they are covered in hoar frost. Beside him sits an old man with snow-white hair in a felt hat who is telling his beads – dried berries from the *dzhida* tree – in sinewy fingers and throwing them down on the white goatskin. As he is does this, he nods his head with a thoughtful air. The powerful Turkman with the forked beard gives him but a cursory glance before once more directing his gaze to the wide ranging steppe through the opening in the yurt.

Now, one of those seated, a lean and wiry Turkman in a striped *chapan*, stirs and raises his head, as if someone had tapped him on the shoulder. He it was who had been assigned to keep in view from early morning the sentinel on the mound. All of a sudden, as if by an inaudible call, the remaining Turkmen in the yurt rouse and lift their heads. They stir, *papakhas* askew and swarthy faces turning towards to the greyhead with the forked beard. Following his gaze, they too fix their eyes on the distance through the latticed frame of the yurt: to the east of the mound, several dark spots are appearing on the shimmering steppe. They seem not to be moving, and yet new spots keep on appearing in places where they had not been earlier. The sentinel on the hill, however, is unconcerned and, as before, remains fixed to his post. The *batyr*, great warrior with the forked beard, continues to watch the skyline in silence, as if admiring it; and now the *papakhas* once more begin sleepily to droop and the hooked noses to peck the air.

Let them take a closer look at the black spots as they move gradually nearer. Now we can make out that they are people. Ah, it is the miserable slaves, Kazakhs taken prisoner by the Turkmen! They were made captive last summer. Since then they have lost their human countenance. It is he – the one with the forked beard and the wiry eyebrows, as if dusted by hoar frost – who led the daring raid on the *aul* of Dyuimkara's tribe and took prisoner the six young women, not yet sixteen, as well as six callow Kazakh youths. These Kazakh girls, six tender beauties, were the proud daughters of the Adai tribe and Dyuimkara's line would be without them forever more. All the males from the Turkmen *aul* Mambetpana, to which the girls had been handed over, had almost lost their heads at the sight of such black-eyed Kazakh girls with their rosy complexions. The burly *dzhigits* from that prosperous *aul* lost their composure at the sight of these prisoners, all but coming to blows over the division of the spoils. It is rumoured to this day that they have still to appropriate our beauties.

A sad tale, a bitter fate!

It was the ruthless abductor, the warrior Zhoneyut – for this is the name of the forked-bearded *batyr* – who had brought back the young male prisoners to his own *aul*. He had summoned his kinsmen and announced his decision. The grey-haired fortune-teller Anadurdy, was despatched to the *aul* of Mambetpana. In exchange for the six young Kazakh girls, let Mambetpana hand over just one young white camel, the very one Kazakh seized during the raid on Khorezm. This young camel was to be sacrificed in memory of the warrior Zhoneyut's younger brother. On the Turkmen steppe his brother had gone by the name of Kekbor, meaning 'ferocious wolf', while his real name was Durdy. Now at his graveside there would be an impressive funeral banquet. Retribution on the Kazakh-Adai, devised by the dead man's older brother, would have been done.

Oh, this revenge will long remain in the memory of the Adai and their blood will run cold at the thought of it.

That very same day, the handsome white camel, only a year old, with its sharply defined humps, has been brought from the *aul* of Mambetpana. Overnight, its legs hobbled, it was left to graze the meadow behind the *aul* where the cattle had not yet been. All night it was guarded by three *dzhigits*.

The Turkmen had been waiting for this funeral banquet and act of vengence for the murder of Kekbor for a whole month now. A caravan set out from the *aul*. The Kazakh boy-prisoners were trussed up with leather belts and sat on humpless dromedaries at the rear of the convoy, hanging their heads and shaking all over. At the front of the caravan, the white hump of the frisky camel flashed by for the last time. The floury dust from the hooves of the Turkmen horses and camels had not yet settled on the road by the time they had arrived at a spot, by wormwood thickets. They had not been travelling long, just enough for a stop to sit down and drink tea. And here the prisoners, strained by the ride, could see at last the mound of earth. The clatter of horseshoes on the road diminished, the dromedaries came to a stop. The Kazakh prisoners on these gaunt animals with haunches as sharp as knives could at last straighten themselves. The bonds had chafed their wrists and ankles to the bone, and the pungent camel sweat had inflamed sores. They were not permitted to dismount and were made to sit for a long time on the camels. One can imagine how these young Kazakh horsemen suffered, not knowing what fate awaited them.

The Turkmen dismounted by the mound forming a tight circle around the grave and, kneeling, began to chant a prayer from the Koran. Holding out their calloused palms, the warriors said their prayers and wiped their faces, the vengeful gleam fleetingly vanishing from their eyes. Silence reigned over the circle in that moment of humility. Not even the clanking of stirrups could be heard – only the muffled voice of the mullah.

When prayers ended, all rose and, with grunts brushed the dust from their knees – a whitish cloud drifted through the gathering and rising skywards, taking with it the recent murmur of prayer. And then the hustle and bustle resumed: the Turkmen fetched the struggling young camel to the south-west side of the grave. The mullah in his white turban came forward and intoned another passage from the Koran. The gathering fell once more to its knees and the warriors, opening their arms, prayed to the Almighty to accept their holy sacrifice. Five *dzhigits*, with sleeves rolled, up-ended the young camel and swiftly and skilfully slaughtered it. Over three freshly-dug holes they erected cauldrons, filled them with water, and lit fires beneath. Smoke from the damp kindling drifted across the steppe rising in brownish wisps.

The Kazakh prisoners finally got down from the dromedaries. It was a familiar enough scene. Smoke rose from the fires, and the folk gathered around for the funeral repast. But were these to have been Kazakh Adai, maybe they would have been more raucous, and things done more briskly. Here, neither loud laughter nor throaty cries were heard; here was no squabbling, no sudden burst of song, no sound of a *dombra* strummed. Where were the flushed *dzhigits*, ardent youngsters circling like predators round a clutch of lissom young women in their finery, waists pulled tight with silken belts of red calico? Not a single yurt had been set up for the funeral banquet. No tinkling of girls' necklaces was to be heard. And as for pure-bred Argamak horses, whose hooves seem barely to touch the dusty road when at full gallop – here the animals languished tethered, their heads fidgeting from the monotony.

All around were the scowling faces of the Turkmen warriors. They had come to the funeral weighed down with their holy books and their sabres, as if afraid to leave them at home where enemies might rush in and steal them.

Here, at last, on great wooden dishes, they have brought in the steaming meat of the young camel. They eat quickly and then begin prayers anew, with a further reading from the Koran. Meanwhile, the captive Kazakhs enter the circle. Each prisoner's arms are held by two hefty warriors. Six grim Turkmen make towards them, sleeves rolled, and daggers drawn. The prisoners look at them with horror and entreaty, but they can detect no shred of pity; the warriors' faces are drawn and heartless. All six raise their daggers as one, to threaten the heads of the prisoners who shrink back white-faced. Their heads fall to their chests in submission to the imminently striking blade. A shudder goes through their bodies.

Yet what followed was a blow with the flat of the blade to the back of the neck of each prisoner which caused all six to recoil and to raise their heads, craning their necks and going rigid. The men forced them to the ground, made them go on all fours and then, grabbing them by the ears, making them lie prostrate with foreheads touching the earth. A Turkman stood above every prisoner and pinned him with his knees. *Kumgani* with long spouts were carried in and water was poured on their heads. Strong fingers dug into the young men's wet hair and began rubbing at the temples, yanking the hair at the back of the head. Then the young men were again made to kneel.

Half-dead with fright, the prisoners could only move their eyes side to side, unable to grasp what was happening. The steel blades, glinting in the midday sun, held to their heads, transfixed their darkened souls. What were these young wretches feeling? The vista of life that once had stretched before them had shunk to a few feet and gone dark. Yet it was the rest of the Turkmen who were frantic to know what was happening. A crowd of them were pressing round the prisoners, eyes gleaming with excitement. The six young Kazakhs were more dead than alive.

Next came the fist of the Turkmen henchman as he struck the back of each head – making them droop even lower. By now, not one of them dared glance around: they froze, so also did the mob. The six henchmen all began to sharpen their knives on the top of their boots, and the sound of it struck terror in the hearts of the kneeling captives.

Now a sharp blade was all but touching each head bent in submission. Slicing back from the forehead through the wet hair, and the keen edge began to lop off each youth's head of hair. Only the rasping scrape of the shaving could be heard. The avid onlookers watched the defenceless heads of the prisoners revealed their smooth and innocent young skin. No one knew what awaited these young men! The barber henchmen finished their task and, wiping the daggers on their jerkins, sheathed them. The shaven-haired prisoners froze on their knees, bending to the ground. Under the burning sun, the defenceless heads seemed already lifeless. The prisoners themselves, exhausted and starving, were on the point of collapsing.

The assembled Turkmen continued to watch in silence. A little to one side, several people were doing something with the hide of the slaughtered young camel. The sleeves of their garments were rolled up and knives gleamed in their hands. Now the crowd began to emit sinister droning noises. Something awful indeed was about to befall. At last the six bearded men labouring over the camel hide had completed their task. The knives sliced the hide into segments which they handed to two old men who tossed it into a tub to soak. The old men then began, painstakingly, to soften the hide with their hands.

Advancing through the crowd towards the prisoners came the warrior Zhoneyut, knowing no fear, feeling no pity. Zhoneyut knows only that under that mound of earth, at which he only briefly glanced, lies his younger brother in an eternal sleep; and he must be avenged.

Kekbor had been a valiant warrior. He had spent his life forever plundering and going on raids. On his grey Argamak horse he made solitary forays into neighbouring Kazakh territories, rounding up their horses and taking captives. It was the Kazakhs who gave him the nickname of Kekbor, Ferocious Wolf, having seen his wolf-like ways. In time, his fellow tribesmen began to call him thus, forgetting the name which had been given him by the mullah. No one remembered that as a child he had been called Durdy.

Kekbor was a veritable wolf: he knew his own strength and would always be the first to attack. He never backed away from danger; he took by force both the glory and the trophies of war. The hangers-on of the wealthy chief of Mambetpana, with whom the warrior Zhoneyut had, at that time, been at odds for several years, had tried to turn his brave and reckless younger brother against him. At any opportunity they would whisper in his ear: 'Heh! Your brother thinks he's such a great fighter. But what is he compared to you? You are the great one, not he!' Upon such words, the blood rushed to the head of proud Kekbor. He indeed envied his brother's renown, strength and valour. It was this envy that drove him into a reckless raid from which he did not return alive.

The Kazakhs, having mustered as a unified force, drove back the Turkmen from the heights of Ustyurt and the plains of Manghistau, and seized the fertile pasturelands of Karyn-Zharyk, Ak-Sorka and Udek. They pushed back the Turkmen onto the dry, barren, sandy plateau which was exposed to the prevailing winds. The many herds from the *aul* of Mambetpana had nowhere to graze, and the Turkmen were worn down by lack of water and constant sandstorms. Their stringed *dutars* gave voice to the lament 'Ailadyr', and the shaman *bakshi*, in shrill tones, bemoaned in song the loss of the fertile pastures of Manghistau.

In the hazy evenings, when the heat was abating and there was a chill in the air, when the mirages were disappearing over the steppe and the outline of the sharp peaks of Kar-Dag was again visible in the north, the Turkmen would come out of their yurts and sit in the shade on their rugs. Over a leisurely meal, sipping at hot tea, they would gaze until their eyes watered towards this land that had been theirs for centuries. Each was silent, but all had the same thoughts.

It was not only the people but the animals too, these dumb beasts, who were irrepressibly drawn to where life had once been good. No matter how vigilantly the Turkmen kept watch on their herds, neither sleeping nor resting, the horses would take advantage of a storm or sudden downpour to take off in droves to the fertile pastures they could still remember. This was how they became such easy prey to the enemy. The obstinate camels likewise knew no restraint, and as soon as the young camels were weaned from their mothers, these, in turn, set off at a fast trot, abandoning the weak offspring, to follow the rest to familiar places where forage had once been plentiful.

The warring Turkmen in their tall *papakhas*, eyes dark with vexation on witnessing all this, conceived a monstrous notion of vengeance upon the enemy, of the utmost cruelty. It would only take one of them to shout: 'Mount your horses, *dzhigits*!' and all would respond in an instant and set off swiftly on a raid. But these constant forays were weakening their people. The moth-eaten *papakhas*, displayed in many a yurt as a sign of mourning for a dead warrior, symbolised for them the losses and deaths of fellow Turkmen tribesmen. Many were the worthy braves lying in unmarked graves. Such deserted graves of glorious warriors – buried somehow, thanks be to God – were now visited only by dogs from nearby Kazakh *auls*.

The Turkmen knew all of this and such misfortune and humiliation preyed on their minds. Yet fewer wished to lock in mortal combat with the enemy.

It was when Kazakh thieves made off yet again with the livestock from the affluent Mambetpana that the *bai* sought out the warrior Zhoneyut and humbly pleaded: 'Help us get back our livestock!' At which the hard-hearted warrior revealed his contempt: 'You have as many kinsmen as ants in an ant hill, and yet you ask me? Round up your *dzhigits* and take them on a campaign. Or would you prefer others to lay down their lives for you? Every one of us, do you not realize, values his life highly.'

So as not to reveal his scorn, the distinguished guest fell silent, as if he had not heard the words of Zhoneyut. Instead, he angrily gripped the handle of his heavy eight-stranded whip.

As was to be expected, the cunning chief of Mambetpana went directly from the warrior Zhoneyut to his younger brother, the headstrong Kekbor, and began to cajole him. Kekbor, guileless and proud, immediately fell for the flattery. Off he set on his own to retrieve the stolen livestock. This was not the first time that Kekbor had single-handedly recaptured the *bai*'s stolen animals. Oh, he was a renowned warrior, the younger brother of Zhoneyut!

Amongst the Kazakhs themselves, the most dangerous and audacious ravager of herds was Dyuimkara, a horseman from the Adai tribe. The horses of the Mambetpana *bai* had no place to hide from him. When it came to plundering and evil deeds, there was none to match him – neither among the Adai nor the Turkmen. His name was long spoken of in folk legends. One of these stories was well known throughout the steppe – it was told time and again, always bringing loud laughter and delight – once the very night of Dyuimkara's honeymoon, the *barymtachi*, (as cattle thieves are known), attacked the *aul* of his bride and made off with much livestock. On hearing the desperate cries of the villagers in all their misfortune, Dyuimkara rose from the conjugal bed, realising at once what had occurred. Breaking away from the embraces of his young bride, he tore out of the yurt, naked as the day he was born, and leaped onto his horse. Just as dawn was breaking, he caught up the *barymtachi* who could see through the twilight that they were being chased by a huge, hairy figure on horseback letting out a terrifying roar and, indeed, completely naked as if it were the devil himself or an avenging angel. A fear as if from beyond the grave seized the plunderers and, beside themselves, they scattered across the steppe, burying their heads in the manes of their horses and abandoning their precious booty.

On his return, around midday, our *batyr* met a rider on the road to the *aul* who lent him a *chapan*. Covering his naked body with it, he brought back the stolen livestock to his father-in-law's enclosure, with not one missing. From that day on, his name alone was enough to strike terror in the hearts of the enemy.

He was powerful, like an irate black camel at the height of its fury. His chest was immensely wide and covered with thick black hair like that of a real *karanar*. In battle he rode about bare-chested on an enormous horse and at the sight of this terrifying *batyr* the enemy invariably took off. Even the Turkmen's half-wild Argamak horses, would recognise him from afar and gather together in tight herds from fright and, with their tails held high, flee over the steppe as if being chased by a pack of wolves.

Many were his Turkmen enemies for he had crossed many in his time – the whole tribe of Mambetpana harboured a grudge against this intrepid Adai who constantly made unexpected raids on their *aul*. Countless were the times that the *bai* had dispatched bands of *dzhigits* to deal with Dyuimkara, only for many of them not to return. More Turkmen warriors had been lost than livestock captured in raids on the Kazakhs.

When Zhoneyut was still a callow youth, a famous reconciliation took place between the two sides at the shrine to the Holy Karaman. Kazakhs and Turkmen gathered to discuss the senseless losses suffered by both sides. These neighbouring tribes had been weakened in the bloody hostilities and, realising this, the Turkmen and the Adai had decided to meet at the tomb of the Holy Karaman. Thousands of *dzhigits* from both sides had gathered and, without dismounting, sullenly and steadfastly stared at one another; remembering old and fresh wounds delivered by the enemy, who had now decided to meet for reconciliation not for combat, and under the bright glare of the sun and not under the cloak of darkness.

The young Zhoneyut, riding to this gathering on the steppe with his grandfather, Ogulen, would remember forever how the Kazakh and Turkmen warriors would resolutely, arrogantly, and implacably scrutinise each other, how the stares of the opponents would meet like the flashing blades of sabres.

The head of the Turkmen was the *biy*, the wise man Zhuma. Leaning back in his saddle with a haughty air, he rode upon his tall grey Argamak horse. Besides the *biy*, slightly to the rear, moving round in circles was a thin, lanky youth on an agile black horse, not unlike a leech. This youth was to become the fat *bai*, Mambetpana, the snake-eyed leader of the large Turkmen tribe.

To begin with, both sides wanted to show off their military daring, so as to remind the enemy of their might and to show that they feared neither battle nor fury. They had come on the pretext of meeting for peace talks, but had, in fact, no intention of begging or humiliating themselves, nor even of bowing their heads before their opponents, they had come to prove they had, in times long gone, been the first to claim the Manghistau land.

The huge *biy*, Zhuma, without changing his haughty position on his high saddle, rode forward on his grey Argamak horse and silently gestured with his horsewhip towards the ancient stone boulder engraved in archaic text which had, over the years, become indecipherable as the surface had become webbed with cracks. The rock had been brought here in times long past and placed on the south-west side of the cemetery, which is sacred for Muslims. Zhuma's confident gesture implied 'Look on, you who have come from afar! Who put this stone here, if not our ancestors?'

But the wise men from the Adai tribe did not lose their heads. A Kazakh *biy* rode out to meet his Turkmen counterpart. With the end of his whip, he too silently pointed to a boulder now sinking almost to the tip into the earth; it was an ancient cracked tombstone, overgrown with henna. Bemused, the Turkmen *biy* gave a sign for two of his mercenaries, one young and one old, to dismount and take a look at the tombstone. The latter approached the stone and silently, with great attention, inspected it from all sides. Then, turning towards their leader, they both shrugged their shoulders, bewildered.

Then it was the turn of the Adai *biy* to signal for his man to go over to their tombstone. The latter approached the gravestone, which protruded unevenly from the ground, and began to pull off the layers of overgrown henna. And there, before the eyes of the *dzhigits,* was revealed the clear and legible image of the Adai seal.

Two Turkmen, leaning over the tombstone, studied it for a long time. Then, silently, they gave Zhuma a look and despondently nodded their heads. The crowd of *dzhigits* surrounding the tombstones started to make guttural noises, some exultant, others indignant, while the horses pranced nervously under them. The Adai let out cries of joy, while the Turkmen *dzhigits* pulled viciously at the horses to subdue them, and then stood silently on the spot shaking their heads with resentment.

The *biy* Zhuma thought he would present conclusive and incontrovertible proof that the Turkmen had owned these lands long before the Adai, and had been the first to place the tombstone. It turned out, however, to be quite the contrary. The older stone over time, almost completely sunk into the earth, preserved the mark of the Kazakh tribe Alshin, who, as is generally known, had settled here much earlier than the arrival of the Turkmen.

At that point, both sides, putting aside for the moment the matter of proof regarding the first ancient settlers, began in loud voices to recount their more recent grudges, stubbornly refusing to back down in their quarrel and accusing one another of cruelty and cunning.

The Turkmen were slandering the Kazakhs, accusing them not only of seizing the best pasture lands, but of constantly stealing their livestock, and kidnapping and raping their young women; the peaceful *auls* had no respite and *dzhigits* were losing their lives. The Adai reminded them that long ago when the wild infidel Zhungari attacked their lands, not only did the Turkmen fail to come to the aid of their fellow Muslims and neighbours, but met them instead with spears and swords when their retreat forced them onto the Turkmen land. The Turkmen, meanwhile, were hoping for the mercy of the foreign invaders. From that time onwards there had been irreconcilable hostility between the Adai and the Turkmen.

The gruff voices of the steppe *dzhigits* rang out for some time. Eventually having declared to each other their grievances, they fell silent. It looked like the reconciliation they had been seeking was not far distant. Wise men from both sides began magniloquently to remind them of things in an effort to quiet the hearts of the *dzhigits* rather than fuel the fire. Speeches by silver-tongued orators resounded. The blessed land of Manghistau is so wide and fertile, they said, that there would be enough space for all the tribes to drive their herds and graze their horses. The land of Manghistau had long given shelter to generations of *batyri*, and in order to live peacefully in this land of plenty, there was no need to bring up the past and renew old scores for the sake of bloody vendettas. The past, they said, should be forgotten, since on the boundless steppe – stretching from Aralsk to Kaspi, from Ustyurt to Kopet-Dag – there is enough room for a happy life for both Turkmen and Kazakhs.

Many an impressive speech was made on both sides. The hunched shoulders of the *batyri* relaxed, and heads were bent down pensively. Dismounting from their horses and forming one throng, Kazakhs and Turkmen alike mounted the sacred hill towards the cave of the Holy Karaman and his ancient tombstone, sacred to both peoples, which rested under the sheer, high rock.

Next to the tombstone, with its overgrown sacred tree covered, according to custom, with different-coloured strips of material, a striped lasso made of plaited horse-hair lay stretched out along the ground: the line of contention, representing the division between the two conflicting sides. The first to make pledges of loyalty and conciliation were those on the Adai side. Then, a five-year-old boy on a black horse appeared and, at full gallop, jumped over the striped lasso. The horse fell with a crash, and the child thrown. He jumped quickly to his feet and, as if nothing had happened, ran off to join his compatriots. Shaken by what they had just seen, the grey-bearded elders on both sides nodded their heads, held their hands to the sky and then wiped them on their beards. They declared unanimously: 'The All-Powerful One does not approve of our conflicts. He forbids further bloodshed. He blames neither Kazakhs nor Turkmen, but He censures senseless hostility which destroys so many brothers of the same faith.'

'Allah is great! Allah is just!' the cry resounded. All called out, from the youngest child to the stooped elders.

And so it was that the Turkmen and Adai swore to live together in friendship and brotherhood, in peace and mutual respect. They took an oath to which the very soul of the Holy Karaman testified.

How many years then passed since that memorable day of reconciliation? The boys who were guarding the horses have long since become fathers; a whole generation has grown to manhood. And what do we see? Did the reconciliation truly bring about a change of heart? Were the dishonest ones not dissembling, those for whom words of faithfulness served to insidiously mask their evil intentions? More and more often it was said among the dishonest that the vows made on the sacred hill had lost their force. And the poisonous words leaked out, first of all, from the affluent Mambetpana tribe, where as a boy Mambetpana had been present at the vow of reconciliation. Then the mullah from the *bai* family of Degeneh-akhun spread the rumour that the Kazakhs had received pardon for their evil deeds by foul play; making false vows at the shrine of Holy Karaman, and now His holy wrath would fall upon them. The Turkmen people, they said, should not forgive the Adai for the many grievances and humiliations brought upon them. They can only make atonement with their blood. 'An eye for an eye, a tooth for a tooth!' screeched the mullah. People heeded his words. The stout *bai* Mambetpana, in particular, was very attentive.

Soon it all started again. The *bai* mercenaries began making raids into the Adai borders to steal their grazing herds. And, of course, the unruly Adai retaliated. *Dzhigits* from both sides seized their *soyili*, the most reliable weapon of the steppe rider, cracking each other's shulls with blows from their clubs – and so it was that blood was once again spilt on the steppe. Old grudges flared up again with the same intensity as before and new grudges were born and took root. Now they no longer fought in open warfare, legion against legion. This time the *batyri* adopted the methods of the wolf and, in a large pack, would attack a lone shepherd and try to kill the weak and defenceless man. They would not only steal herds of horses, but maim the herdsmen and cut off their heads with pole-axes; in reciprocal attacks, *dzhigits* would vandalise the holy graves of the their enemy's ancestors. At this point, those who had firmly upheld the great reconciliation; those who had not wanted to get involved in the renewed hostility, which had reached its nadir: they could hold out no longer. And so, axes swinging, they rushed to join the fight. Even those *batyri* most faithful to their pledge, like Zhoneyut, were obliged to mount their horses for battle.

A word of reason can extinguish enmity, yet a word of malice can fan the flame. If a spear pierces a quarrel, then only the words of a wise man can separate vicious opposition. A wise man alone can inspire the human heart to give way to peace, whereas a wicked fool can only swing his club and incite murder.

Few are the wise men on this earth, and many are the fools; wise men are seen just once in a thousand years, whereas fools are born each day. It is still not known whether people will heed the words of the wise or whether, once armed, they will follow those stupendous fools. The simplest thing is to settle scores: if someone strikes you, you strike them back; if someone threatens to murder you, you murder them. Then, when the enemy has attacked and the clash of swords is heard from afar, and the sparks of metal are flying; then the know-all who called for peace will be cursed.

This was the conclusion that Zhoneyut had come to, and once again he mounted his horse for battle. Once he had made up his mind and picked up his weapon, there was no stopping this formidable warrior. With his hair flying, he rode off into battle on his faithful Argamak horse.

Chapter II

Dyuimkara, the Adai *batyr*, too was unable to stand by and watch as the others reached for their knives, cudgels and *soyili*. It was not enough for this violent Kazakh *batyr* to steal cattle and the Turkmen horses; in response to the atrocities of his neighbours, he began to retaliate in an even more cruel fashion. He would plunder Turkmen *auls* causing grave insult to strict Muslims. His actions and orders were truly merciless.

Once the warrior Zhoneyut came across on his travels a familiar *aul* spread out on the gentle slopes of a mountain ridge. He found all the villagers wailing with grief; women tearing at their hair and howling and sobbing. Zhoneyut soon discovered what terrible things had befallen these people.

He was led to the edge of the *aul* to a ditch trampled down by a flock of sheep. Huddled together, two dozen girls were either sitting or lying down in the dust and manure. With scratched faces and torn dresses they beat at the ground, letting out pitiful moans. They told Zhoneyut what had happened. As he stood and listened quietly an ominous look began to appear in his eyes.

Once a year, during the festival of Kurban-Ait, the Turkmen allow themselves to forget about their daily tasks and worries and there is merriment all around. This year the men had set off for the *aul* of Mambetpana where there were to be horse races while the women remained alone in their *aul* and played games, sang songs, danced, and sat on the huge swings they had put up.

Making the most of the men's absence on the day of merrymaking and revelry, Dyuimkara and his band burst upon the village like a pack of wolves. Ignoring divine and ancient traditions, the Adai horsemen, charging by, cut the ropes of the swings with their swords and lashed at the defenceless women with their whips. Then they rounded up the prettiest girls and young women and led them to the edge of the *aul*. There in the ditch, which had been trampled by sheep, they violated them. Having assuaged their animal lust, the thugs from Dyuimkara's band went on to jeer at the women's loss of honour. They pulled up the hems of their dresses and tied them round their heads, and then scattered their helpless naked bodies with dust and ash.

When they found out about the attack, the mounted Turkmen raced back to the *aul*, but Dyuimkara's thugs were miles away by then. When they returned they found the shamed women – daughters, wives, sisters, brides-to-be – prostrate on the ground weeping. The *dzhigits'* eyes flashed darkly, and they stood, not having the courage to lift their heads, holding onto their horses' reins. They did not dare go into their yurts, for dreadful assumptions had rooted them to the spot.

Then the warrior Zhoneyut arose as if from a deep slumber. How would his people live on this earth now that they had been made outcasts? While his pride had been a fleet-footed Turkmen Argamak horse, his joy and honour had been his daughters' chastity. All that had now been taken away; all had been ridiculed. How could he now look his children in the eye? No! There had to be an end to all this.

The warrior Zhoneyut turned his horse around, gave a flick of his whip and rode off towards the north.

At first, he did not hear the sound of hooves behind him, but when he looked around, he saw that the men from the disgraced *aul* had caught up with him. From that day forth, Zhoneyut hardly ever dismounted from his horse. He headed one Turkmen raid after another, the men seething with resentment as they sought out the despised Adai, Dyuimkara. But this *batyr* was not easily frightened. He began to carry out more bold and cruel acts. This previous summer he had chased a band of Turkmen single-handedly, making off with their horses. The brutal Dyuimkara had been so carried away with his capture that he had not noticed that he strayed over the boundaries of Kokpakta. It was already dark by the time he realised that he had wandered far off course, so he decided to pass the night in a small yurt which stood by the foot of a hill on the steppe. It turned out to be the camp of a lone Chaban-Turkman.

Who could fathom why the reckless Dyuimkara would, all of a sudden, choose to spend the night with a sworn enemy? Maybe the Adai warrior was relying on the old steppe custom whereby any guest entering a house is believed to be a visitor from God and, therefore, sacred and not to be insulted. Maybe he was hoping that his notoriety had gone before him, and was certain that the owner of the yurt would not dare to lay a finger on him. It is known of old that these mighty men are carefree and naïve as children.

He was warmly welcomed by the owner but, when Dyuimkara left the yurt to bathe, the Turkman poured warm tar into the *batyr's* sheath. They say that the Turkman's wife, terrified, grabbed at her husband's hands as if to say, 'What are you doing? Even though he is a scoundrel and a low-life dog, this one is still our guest!' At which the Turkman silently and with growing fury pushed his wife aside. When the Adai returned to the yurt, he sprawled out without a care in the world and fell fast asleep. At this, the Turkman sent off the messenger boy to the *aul* of Mambetpana. The *bai* then quickly despatched his messenger to Kekbor.

And so it came to pass that the stern warrior, Zhoneyut, stood looking at his brother's grave, surveying those who gathered round him, and twisting in his hands pieces of hide from the young white camel. There they were, standing in front of him, the heads of the Mampetpana and, as usual, at the centre of the throng were the fat *bai* and the mullah

Degen-akhun. Turning his sweaty face towards the mullah, the *bai* Mambetpana was staring with a bored look at the mouth of Degen-akhun as he murmured his eternal prayer and picked at the hem of the white silken turban. Around these two, the men in their shaggy *papakhas* half sang along to the words of the prayer and half nodded off. Only the stout figure of the *bai* Mambetpana, as if on a stroll and not at a graveside, had failed to bow his head: nor had he covered his arrogant face with his hands. With his flabby double chins and snide look, his narrow eyes stared in the distance.

This *bai* was as arrogant as he was devious. He had the cunning of a fox. Mambetpana could be genial and courteous when he wanted to be, with formidable figures like the unsuspecting *batyr,* Kekbor. Yes, he could be both when the frown had cleared from his brow, his flabby double chins and stout belly, grown soft by sweet caresses, had merged as one, and he was ready to enfold someone in an embrace. Such deftness from one so hefty! What supple and expressive hands he has! How adroit and ingratiating when he wants to bestow his *bai* favour on the right person! The warrior Zhoneyut can imagine in what grovelling tones the *bai* would speak to Kekbor: 'Now, *batyr*, the hour of your great deed has come. You are the most powerful and unbeatable among us, and glory will be yours when you imprison that Kazakh dog, Dyuimkara. Go and get him, Kekbor, he is almost within your grasp. There won't be another opportunity like this. Go, illustrious warrior. Rid your people of this audacious marauder, who has affronted all of us!'

Now everyone knows what happened: the crafty Mambetpana had concealed the news that the Adai's sheath had been filled with tar. The cunning *bai* knew full well that honest, brave Kekbor would not go into combat in such an uneven contest. He knew also that without such an advantage the imprudent, courageous Kekbor would be unlikely to get the better of the mighty Adai, Dyuimkara, that terrible *shaitan*, possessed as he was with an evil spirit.

The warrior Zhoneyut reflected on this, all the while surveying the *bai* and his entourage with resentment.

So the cheery Dyuimkara, refreshed by a good night's sleep, drank his morning tea and set off, leaving behind the yurt of the hospitable Turkman. Having reached the ancient holy shrine he noticed a cloud of dust in the distance which was moving quickly towards him. Thinking it was part of the herd, he reined in his tall black and white piebald stallion and waited. As his pursuer got nearer and Dyuimkara could finally see him clearly, the Adai unhurriedly dismounted, climbed up a small hill, and began to unfasten his trousers. As Kekbor approached, the audacious Dyuimkara bared his behind and crouched down to perform his morning function. The grey Argamak on which the Turkman was seated came to a stop and, rearing on the spot with white foam frothing from its mouth, almost collided with the wide back of the unruffled *batyr*. Now on his haunches, he was relieving himself in the cold morning wind.

'Heh, Dyuimkara, is that you? Get up this minute, you brute!'

The Adai, however, seemed not to have heard him. Nonchalantly he began to dig a hole before him with the handle of his horsewhip. He picked out a clump of grass with which, half rising, he wiped himself clean. He got up slowly, fastened his trousers and tightened them. Turning only then, he asked the traveller in a calm voice what he wanted.

In the meantime both stallions, standing side by side, gave each other wild looks and shook their heads angrily, flattening back their ears. Dyuimkara clapped his hands, shaking the dirt from them, and then wiped his palms on his trousers. His robe was open at the chest and thick wiry hair poked out.

The rider on the grey Argamak shook with indignation. He held a curved sabre in his hand. Dyuimkara calmly went to his horse and he mounted without haste. One might have thought he was about to offer the traveller some tobacco.

'Ah, you cursed Kazakh! Prepare for a duel!' exploded Kekbor, flying into a rage.

'Do you really want to do battle with me, my fellow?' Dyuimkara asked calmly.

'Swords at the ready!' said the Turkman *batyr* in a hoarse voice.

'As you wish,' replied the Adai.

'I am going to knock off that iron head of yours, Kazakh!' threatened Kekbor.

'Come now, you can do better than that, you whelp,' responded Dyuimkara. 'I'll show you how it should be done.'

The battle-horses, sensing the growing tension of their masters, pulled against their bridles. A terrible change came over the *batyri* themselves: they held each other in a long stare; no one moved. Dyuimkara sat in his saddle confidently as if he was indeed thinking of offering his opponent some tobacco, instead of preparing for battle. Neither did the *batyr* Kekbor, a fearless warrior, show any signs of alarm. With his mighty arm he held back his fierce Argamak, deliberating when and how to take the first thundering strike.

Boundless desolate steppe! So marvellous at this early hour of day! You have no longer the strength to stop these *batyri* and quench their desire for bloodshed. There is no one to stop them, calm them, bring them to reason. A little chirping bird, a steppe lark, flew around the heads of the *batyri*. Frightened out of its nest, it flew from the bushes with a call of alarm, as if beseeching them to make peace.

Not far from the *batyri* now circling each other, a herd of graceful deer made for a watering place. When they saw the over-excited horses and their fierce riders, the timid animals were struck with fear. The two *batyri* noticed neither lark nor deer, for they were locked in their battle fury. They were aware only of each other: two people preparing to fight to the death. Death waited eagerly for one of them, and Death it was that transformed their faces. Their brows furrowed menacingly; their eyes narrowed; their cheekbones seemed more pronounced, as if chiselled. A nerve twitched in their powerful jawbones. Their eyes were bloodshot for in their veins the thick, angry blood, the blood of warriors, was boiling over.

The silver Argamak of the Turkman reared up sharply and jumped forward. A gleaming sword sliced the air. The piebald stallion of the Kazakh recoiled and the Turkman's blow was foiled. Kekbor pulled down his woollen *papakha* tightly: it was not in his nature either to cheat or retreat during a fight. He prepared to lunge, and only then did Dyuimkara reach for his sword. But what was this? Normally, he would unsheath his mightly sword in a moment. But the blade would not come out of its sheath! Without taking his watchful eyes off his opponent, he tried again and again to pull out his weapon, but it would not surrender to his hand.

Do you know what the cold hand of death is like? How the chill of death pierces through you from the roots of your hair to the soles of your feet? Perspiration covered the wide brow of the *batyr* Dyuimkara. His throat went dry and the taste in his mouth was as bitter as wormwood. As if poisoned by a snake, his eyes and soul were plunged into darkness.

Kekbor's shining blade flashed once more past Dyuimkara's head. On an impulse, he undid his belt from his sword and raised it, along with the sheath, above his head, over the flattened ears of the piebald stallion. And there followed Kekbor's mighty blow. A terrible ringing resounded, as if thunder rumbled over Dyuimkara's head. He just had time to lower his sheathed sword and glance around, when he noticed lying on the ground the two fragments of Kekbor's sword that had broken in his hand. The mighty *batyri* looked down at these fragments and ground their teeth. Then they set their horses on each other. The battle-horses, snorting and baring their teeth, drew nearer; the steel stirrups banged together, and the *batyri* began to wrestle. They no longer had any use for swords or even horsewhips. The *batyri* grabbed hold of each other tightly and, pressing down in the stirrups, tried somehow to knock or pull their opponent from his horse. The Argamak horses, buckling under the weight of the mighty men, moaned and gasped for breath. It seemed as if the *batyri* would crush their horses into the ground; that they would show no mercy either for their steeds or for each other.

As bloodsucking ticks leech upon human skins, so the men gripped each other tightly. On hearing the sound of tearing clothes and the deep-throated roars of the *batyri*, the battle-horses were terrified. But the men had lost their heads and were not thinking of their horses – in fact, they had forgotten about everything, in the throes of their mortal struggle. The grey Argamak began to whinny for all the steppe to hear, rearing up on its hind legs. A piece of flesh had been ripped from its mane with a tearing sound, and a deep shudder ran through its body. With its last drop of strength it shrank back. A sharp tug on the reins pulled at the horse, and when it looked round it saw that two men were lying on the ground, and that one of those men was its master.

The men were wrestling furiously, first one and then the other on top. Not far from them lay the shattered sword, gleaming faintly in the dust, and each of the fighters wanted to to reach it first. First one *batyr* seemed likely to lay his mighty hand on the sword, and then the other; but then they rolled over in the other direction and the fragmented sword remained where it was on the dusty grass of the steppe.

The wrestling bodies were intertwined on the ground, but the reins of the grey horse remained in its master's hand causing the animal to be jerked from side to side. Suddenly the grey Argamak felt a sharp blow across its nostrils. Coiling like a snake, the tip of the whip had lashed the horse across its muzzle, causing it almost to fall onto its back. Having righted itself, it stood and watched as its master lay dying, defeated by his opponent. The massive black Colossus, his bare chest covered all over in camel-like hair, was sitting on top of his master and was tying his hands with a length of rein.

The Adai had managed after all to reach the fragment of his enemy's weapon. In one stroke, Dyuimkara cut off the end of the rein which was held tightly in the Turkmen's fist. Then he tied his opponent's hands behind his back. The defeated fighter lay on the ground, barely conscious from exhaustion. The Adai beckoned his horse, cut loose the bridle, and began to tie up the defeated Kekbor's feet. Kekbor had by this time come round. An enraged and pitiful cry resounded through the steppe. He called to his comrades for help, but no answer came. Only a lark could be heard, somewhere on high. In the silence, Dyuimkara, unruffled and businesslike, continued to tie Kekbor's feet with the reins, wiping the sweat from his brow every now and again.

The grey Turkmen Argamak, eyes protruding, rolled around nearby desperate to get nearer to its master, but not daring to. Towering above him was the dark expanse of Dyuimkara's curved back. Stooping, he inspected the surrounding area of the steppe as if looking for something, or perhaps fearing the arrival of enemies. But unable to find anything in particular, Dyuimkara scratched his hairy chest with the handle of the horsewhip which he had picked from the ground.

He noticed several stones sticking out of the ground not far off, gravestones of an ancient shrine. An idea struck him, and Dyuimkara raised himself heavily from the ground, seized the sword fragment and set off in the direction of the cemetery.

The gravestones were covered with henna, which was beginning to turn black. Beside them was a deep ravine in the earth from a fallen tombstone, in which human remains could be seen as well as a yellow skull. Maybe the grave had been plundered by jackals. Dyuimkara stood by the edge of the grave meditatively still scratching at his hairy body with the handle of the horsewhip. Then he returned to Kekbor, who was lying on the ground with his arms and legs bound. On seeing his enemy approach, Kekbor gave a huge roar. The Adai growled contemptuously, and grabbing him by the collar dragged him off towards the gravestones. Only the dust rose on the last ignominious journey of the Turkmen *batyr*.

Dyuimkara set down the prisoner by the grave, leaving him lying on the ground while he rested for a moment or two. Then he bent over, grabbed hold of him and lifted the bulky *batyr* high above his head as if he were a small child. Staggering a little, he hurled the prisoner into the grave. A thick cloud of dust arose. Dyuimkara took a step back. From the depths of the old tomb came the sound of deep wailing; and it seemed not the wails of a man, but those of a corpse from beyond the grave. Hearing the cries, the grey Argamak approached loudly, and began circling the tomb as if it had lost its mind. Dyuimkara – who was covered in white dust from the grave – began to fill the grave with clumps of earth. Then, heaving stones from the ground with his immense strength, he began to hurl them into the tomb. The dying man's cries abated. One last, weak groan was heard, and then all quiet. At this the grey Argamak gave a wild, sorrowful neigh in response and with a stamp of its hooves raced off in the direction of its master's *aul*.

When the horse galloped into the *aul* without its rider and the saddle hanging loosely at one side, those who had long been expecting the *batyr* Kekbor realised that something awful had happened to him. The Turkmen mounted their horses and set off to search for a body. On the following day the band of riders, led by Zhoneyut, came across the old tombstone, heaped with fresh earth. Above the grave, scattered haphazardly with earth, huge black flies swarmed around in a dense cloud. The Turkmen dismounted and looked into the hole. What they saw there made their hearts fill with horror. At the bottom of the grave lay the body of Kekbor. On his chest lay a large stone; his body was barely covered with earth and flies crawled all over his face. Kekbor's sword fragment had been tossed to the ground by the side of the grave. Those Turkmen who knew about the affair of Dyuimkara's tar-filled sheath, guessed immediately that the ferocious Adai had not even killed his opponent with a sword, but had overpowered him in hand-to-hand combat and had trussed him up while he was alive and thrown him into the tomb.

Now the warrior, Zhoneyut, the dead man's older brother, standing by the grave, swore that to his dying day, he would mercilessly take vengeance on Dyuimkara himself and all his tribe and heirs.

It was soon after that, at the funeral banquet by Kekbor's grave, that the Turkmen gathered to slaughter the white camel yearling. The warrior, Zhoneyut, stood as if turned to stone, looking at the earthen mound where his brother lay at rest. He turned round to see the six Turkmen in woolly *papakhas*, holding pieces of camel hide, moving through the crowd towards the six Kazakh prisoners. The old Turkmen, with rolled-up sleeves, came and stood opposite the shaven-headed youths; then each Turkman grabbed the prisoner opposite him by the ears and made him kneel before him. The *dzhigits* who were assisting them handed over the hides which were slammed down, each one, on the shaven heads. The hide was still warm, damp and soft, and stuck immediately to the youths' warm bare heads. Not realising what was happening, the prisoners looked around with terrified, child-like eyes. In the meantime the six elderly Turkmen skilfully worked their fingers across and carefully smoothed down and tucked in the edges of the hide, as if they were covering the bare heads with round hats. Next they pulled out leather straps and wound them tightly round the edges of the hide. They pulled them fast which caused the prisoners' heads to ache and their temples to pound, becoming unbearably painful.

After this sinister ritual, the Kazakh prisoners were put once again on the humpless camels; then the crowd remounted their horses and the whole procession made its way back to the *aul*. The dust arose from the hooves of camel and horse and the sun beat down intolerably. The pungent camel sweat poured into the prisoners' eyes, but they were unable to wipe it away for their hands were bound. With the sun at its zenith, the suffering of the martyrs, whose torture was on show for all to see, was intense. The pitiless crowd of steppe-dwellers jostled closer to get a better look at the torture and out of curiosity the *dzhigits* came over one by one to view the sufferers' distorted faces. This journey to the *aul* seemed to the prisoners as if it would take them to the world's end.

The faded plateau was lost in the delirium of a shimmering haze in which appeared here and there dark mountains of monstrous proportions. But close up they turned out to be only random thorny briars.

The skin of the bent necks of the camels, had been chafed like old leather belts, and was covered in gleaming sweat that ran down the thin camel hair. The burning heat had become intolerable even for the camels. Under the scorching sun, the terrible, excruciating pain – unbearable for anyone – in the heads of the tortured men got worse with each moment. The raw camel hide, pulled fast on the shaven heads of the prisoners, began to tighten and compress their brains, and they felt that their skulls were cracking under the strain. One of the Kazakh prisoners cried out in desperation, and losing all reason began to beat his head on the back of the prisoner sitting in front of him.

The six prisoners, in their torment, gradually began to lose all human countenance, that which was given by You. Their faces became disfigured and a salty liquid ran from their eyes and nostrils which they were unable to wipe away because of their fettered hands. The clang of the iron fetters was unremitting because the bodies of the prisoners were convulsed with interminable agony. On seeing all this (oh, what inhumanity!) the steppe *dzhigits* triumphantly circled the cortège on their horses doing fancy tricks, with raucous cries: 'Oh, *araukhi*, vengeance has been wreaked!' They then took off at full speed in the direction of the *aul*, kicking up the dust behind them. Only two bearded Turkmen, who were escorting the convoy of prisoners, stayed behind. The unearthly cries, the grinding of teeth, the wild laughter and madness – this is what the luckless prisoners had come to, doomed to be *mankurti*.

Their wailing and cries were heard in the *aul* for a whole week. Then all six fell silent. Their hair, flattened by the dried camel hide, had begun to grow back into the head and was penetrating the brains of the young men, which caused them to lose their memory and their wits. The *mankurti*, the name that is given to the prisoners, had already forgotten who they were or where they had come from, and had begun to behave like animals: they lost the power of speech and they took to eating the wild grass of the steppe. They grazed alongside the camels behind the *aul*, and in the evening they returned to the *aul* with the herd and lay down for the night with the animals. Oh, Allah! It even happened that they degraded themselves further, committing sins with one another.

Zhoneyut sent back two of the *mankurti* to the Adai in order that they could see how the Turkmen avenge their enemies. Four remained by the *aul* and continued to live out their twilight existence, wandering over the steppe with the herd and gathering dry *kizyak,* the dung from the cattle to make fuel with. This they were still able to do.

It so happened that, after a period of time, these four prisoners appeared near the pointed burial mound used by the sentinel and on which the stake had been driven into the ground. The watchman stood surveying the distant enemy lands. Yet he paid no attention to them since they were no longer the enemy but limp, frail ghosts of their former selves. They arrived at the *aul* and from their sacks they poured out onto a heap the *kizyak* which they had gathered.

Chapter III

That raid – so terrible for the Kazakhs – on the *aul* of Dyuimkara's tribe, when the young men and women were taken prisoner, was the last of the warrior Zhoneyut's campaigns.

For the first time, he reflected on the fact that the Yer-Oglan tribe, renowned for its many great *batyri*, no longer boasted any outstanding warriors capable of leading fighters in military campaigns. Some had died and none had been born to replace them. It was a long time since Zhoneyut himself had had to take up a spear or sword to prove his military might in one-to-one combat. Time waits for no man. The time had come to think about picking someone – a younger and a stronger man – to stand beside him in order to lead the Turkmen into campaigns and to defend their people from enemies. These thoughts ate away at Zhoneyut. The limits of his strength, of which until then he had been unaware, he could now feel in the depths of his old heart. He could no longer gauge what he could or could not accomplish. Now he knew that only his great reputation for boundless might and strength remained, and that most of his life had already passed.

He had had a son by the name of Klych, who was as powerful and thickset as a steppe *saksaul* plant, and who had no equal when it came to using a weapon. He trounced everyone in duels using either swords or spears; when it came to arrows he was an excellent marksman, and held a sabre with great force. However, he was still young and inexperienced when he was put into brutal combat, and had ardently sacrificed his life in battle. Now he is laid to rest in the family grave behind the *aul*.

He had a second son, Alpan, who was brash, fearless and recklessly brave; who was feared by all his contemporaries. As a child he was barely standing when he waved his fists to strike anyone whom he disliked, whether it be a neighbour's son or a stray dog. When he grew older and received his first horse, he would often gallop out onto the steppe chasing some enemy or other and flog them mercilessly with his child's horsewhip. He grew into an incredibly daring and obstinate *dzhigit* who would fly into a rage in an instant. Moreover, when he heard of an argument or brawl, he would make straight for it with bravado. He loved with all his heart his loud, fiery Uncle Kekbor, who would do all he could to indulge him and always chose him over the others.

On one distant campaign led by his uncle, Alpan met his death in a foreign land and was buried in an unmarked grave. Perhaps he was not even buried and instead the animals and birds of prey made off with his bones, for no trace of him was ever found.

Zhoneyut's youngest son, the last-born and the favourite, did not rush off to fight on campaigns, nor did his father make him go. Daulet grew into a dignified, broad-shouldered *dzhigit* with beautiful, soft brown eyes. Gentle, compliant, and always with a smile (despite this he looked formidable) it is said of such strapping men that they can pick up and carry a *dzhigit* on each shoulder. Daulet was kind-hearted and had a gentle disposition, yet once, on a day of festivities, he wrestled everyone to the ground and there was no one left to beat him amongst all the burly contestants. This he did without resorting to anger, and keeping a smile on his face. With large eyes and a wide, high forehead, a fair face, which was unusual amongst the dark-skinned Turkmen, Daulet's cheeks would flush bright red whenever he was pleased or moved. His radiant eyes would shine warmly, and he was adored by everyone. Being tall, striking and well-built, with thick eyebrows, he did not look at all intimidating. Even the ferocious dogs of the *aul* – Turkmen Alsatians and Wolfhounds – would wag their tails on seeing Daulet, and would come and make a fuss of him and sit at his feet.

Daulet was popular with the girls and young women, for he was very affectionate with them and chose to spend his time in their company. His father had heard about this but said nothing until he discovered, one day, that his son was making regular visits to a young widow whose husband had recently died on campaign. Zhoneyut summoned his son to him and rebuked him severely. This was the first time that Zhoneyut had expressed disapproval of his youngest son's behaviour. In other matters, Zhoneyut paid no heed at all.

Zhoneyut's lenient attitude towards his son caused resentment in the steadfast warrior, Kekbor, which bubbled over like boiling water in a cauldron whenever Daulet's name came up. Moreover, although his uncle was not known for his wit – and most of the family knew this – no one dared to contradict him. Kekbor, keeping close counsel with the mullahs and wealthy men of the *aul*, thought that it was for his intelligence and quick wits that he was respected. He did not conceal his contempt for his nephew, considering him an idle lad, and whenever he saw him he would try and pick a fight with him. What particularly enraged Kekbor was that his nephew would always remain calm and serene: his beautiful large eyes would have a smile in them and he would simply colour a little. It was the flushed cheeks and womanly eyes that incensed the warrior Kekbor even more. He was never able to retaliate when his nephew made an apt or cutting remark, and could only roar thunderously like a camel and use foul language.

What particularly incensed him was that this strapping lad, instead of seeking fame in battle or in raids on the neighbouring enemy by stealing their horses or livestock, preferred to spend all his time playing the *dutar*. Kekbor considered that this brought shame upon the whole male species. Only a good-for-nothing would choose to play their *dutar* instead of learning, like a true warrior, how to handle a spear or a sword. If a man was incapable of this, said Kekbor, then he should pick up a crook and go and graze cattle on the steppe.

Daulet had spent his childhood around *dutar* players and *bakshi* singers. By the time he was fifteen he had taught himself to play the *dutar* so well that he became renowned amongst the musicians of the steppe. He became a skilful and masterful player of the *dutar*. You have probably been told how the famous *dutar* player from Tatauza, Yakhiya, was enthralled on hearing the young Daulet play.

The warrior Zhoneyut, often on campaigns where he would spend days on end in the saddle, considered that revelry and merrymaking were a matter for old women and young girls, and tried whenever he could to avoid such things. So it was he never came to see his son performing in front of an audience. Daulet never dared to play on the *dutar* when his father was around. Out of all the family, the only admirer of his musical gifts was the elder, Anadurdy. Zhoneyut knew of his son's passion but in his heart did not approve of it, considering it a trivial fondness for amusement.

And so it happened that, several years earlier, when the great reconciliation was still in place, Anadurdy set off to visit the Kazakhs for a *dutar* competition and took Daulet with him. There, the young musician enthralled the audience with his skill, and competing with the best musicians of Manghistau excelled, winning, coming joint first place with a young Kazakh *Kiuishi*. Anadurdy was so proud: as they say, it was as if another *papakha* had grown on his head. When he returned home, he told everyone about the young Daulet's achievement and many were overjoyed. Even the stern Zhoneyut seemed proud of his son, but said nothing. But what of his uncle Kekbor? He went white with rage and immediately rode off to see his brother; on entering the house, he refused even to go through to the place of honour, but instead sat on the thick felt by the entrance. He began hurriedly to criticise and castigate his nephew who had, it was said, brought shame on his family by going to a festival hosted by their age-old enemies and a mob of brawlers and *dutar* players. What disgrace! What degradation!

'Your son is a *dutar* player! A *dutar* player! Do you understand what that means?' he ranted. 'These *bakshi* with their shamanism, and these singers and *dutar* strummers – what good will come of it all? The enemy fears only the fighter on horseback in a sheepskin *papakha* with a spear in his hand. And what of these *bakshi*? And the *Kiuishi*? Are they *dutar* players? People regard them as fools and they are feared by no one. From time immemorial every man from the Yer-Oglan tribe has struck fear into the hearts of the Adai. And what do we have here? Nothing but humiliation! Tell me, brother, tell me honestly – did he frighten even one puny Kazakh? Take a look at the size of the lad! He does nothing but talk, and has probably been bewitched by a *shaitan* or a genie, which has made him weak and changed him from a fighter into a woman. He stayed with the Adai a whole month, handing over his weapons and brushing aside his soldier's honour and all the grudges between our tribes. He made merry with our enemies as if they were his brothers born of the same woman. What disgrace! What dishonour! Even a woman would not humiliate herself in such a way.

'Just take a look at Daulet, almost bursting with pride from his visit with the Adai; as if he had returned home from a successful military campaign bearing trophies. And as for that Anadurdy, empty-headed fool he is, slapping his thighs with glee! You should have heard him. "When our young Daulet started to play on his *dutar*, those Kazakhs, our lifelong enemies, were clicking their tongues in appreciation." What a thing to brag about! What's there to be proud of? He would have been better off sitting over a goatskin and telling fortunes with his *dzhida* berries. Instead of those good-for-nothings, we could have sent a Turkmen *batyr* who would have kicked up a right fuss and you wouldn't have seen them nodding their heads and clicking their tongues then! All those *Kiuishi, bakhshi* and *dutar* players – they are not real men! They are worse than women melting at the first tender look from a *dzhigit*; worse than stray bitches. A spear and a sword are what is needed to build up the reputation of our people, not the wailing of the *bakhshi* and the strumming of a *dutar*.

'When I met him yesterday and gave him a lecture he actually grinned at me and replied: "What are you making a fuss about, Uncle? Why are you ranting and raging like boiling water in a cauldron? Well, so what if you have set upon the Adai, have killed a few *dzhigit* and had frightened away a stud of horses? What of it? Would it have dented your honour, Uncle, if you had spared these *dzhigit* their lives and had left the horses to graze on the grassland?"

'What has your son come to, saying these things to me?

'I began to tell him of the glorious feats of our forefathers, but his only response was to laugh! "There's no need to disturb our forefathers, Uncle," he said, "since no one has wronged them. They died and killed men in the process." Just think what that good-for-nothing said to me! As if to say, just leave our ancestors in peace from now on. Eh? How do you like that then?'

Zhoneyut listened patiently to his brother and then sent for his son. Kekbor left, deciding not to wait for his nephew. On seeing him out, Zhoneyut said to his affronted brother: 'Well, what do you expect from him? He's still only a lad, you know. He'll come to reason when he gets a bit older.'

Kekbor darted like an arrow from the yurt, and from that day until his death at the hands of Dyuimkara he had never set foot in his older brother's house. He was mortally offended; he had not had the response from Zhoneyut that he sought.

As for Daulet, he continued to live his life as carefree as before. Right up to the death of Kekbor, Zhoneyut did not obstruct his only remaining son in any way.

After the funeral banquet at his brother's graveside, when the guests had feasted on the sacrificed young camel and departed, Zhoneyut summoned Daulet. As master of the house, he dismissed everyone from the yurt in order to be alone with his son for the night. Through the open lattice, the night sky could be seen patterned with the trajectories of shooting stars. Through the gaps in the yurt came the song of crickets.

Somewhere on the edge of the *aul*, in a neglected earthen hovel, languished the six Kazakh prisoners, howling in unbearable pain. Their cries resounded through the night. Sometimes one of them would take to roaring and yelping like an animal, and the terrible grinding of teeth was as thunder in the evening air. The handcuffs clanked and rattled as one of them beat himself about the head, covered tightly with dry camel hide.

Hearing these awful sounds, no one in the *aul* could get to sleep. The tethered horses flattened back their ears in fright, stretching their necks in the direction of the howling and whining. Even the camels did not lie down, but stood with their massive dark bodies looming up in the darkness, their heads ceasing for a moment their endless chewing of the cud.

Daulet lay silently in the dark of the yurt. Zhoneyut was quiet too. The son lay on the felt rag, his back turned to the wall, legs curled up close to his chest. The father waited to see what Daulet would do next.

Along the mountain ridge of the *aul*, it was a chilly night. A cold wind came down from the hills, and soon Zhoneyut began to shiver. Not a sound could be heard except the heart-wrenching cries from the hovel. The prisoners were gradually losing their minds; no longer aware of anyone, or of what was happening around them. Zhoneyut had stationed armed guards by the hovel, and their deep voices rang out from time to time trying to quieten the wailing. But the prisoners could no longer see reason, and so the *aul* knew no rest.

Zhoneyut raised himself and glanced over to his son, and suddenly noticed that his shoulders were shaking. What was this? Could he really be crying? Indignation made the father rise from his bed. At his uncle's graveside, Daulet had stood dry-eyed and stony-faced. Could he show more pity for the prisoners than for his fearless uncle, whose horrific death was the reason for this awful vendetta? Kekbor was right to have been so outraged: the music, the cursed *dutar*, and the merry jaunts and songs had cast from his son all the fighting spirit; his soldier's honour and the notion of what it was to be a real man. Daulet had forgotten what a sacred thing vengeance was, forgotten his duty to his illustrious forefathers: not worth the sheepskin of a soldier's *papakha*. It would have been better to emasculate him to, look upon him as one of the cowardly women! How could he lie there and sob from pity at the wailing of those debased beasts.

Zhoneyut lay back on the pillows, pulling the quilt tightly around him. The night was a cold one. He had still not made up his mind whether to speak to his son.

The next morning Daulet rose early. Later, Zhoneyut summoned his son to take tea with him. Daulet, when he appeared looked somewhat put out. His face was pinched and pale; he had dark blue circles under his eyes. He silently poured tea for his father and himself from the striped urn, but did not touch his own bowl. Zhoneyut sipped his tea and gave his son stern glances from beneath bushy brows. The father could read on his son's face the reason for his silence, but he felt incapable of saying anything to him.

A few days later Zhoneyut was setting off on a hunt and, for the first time, invited his son along with him. They took with them only two experienced, wiry foxhounds. The warrior looked at his son: despite all the insults and scorn that his brother had heaped on Daulet, the father felt that before him stood someone obstinate and headstrong. He had witnessed Daulet's audacious way of speaking and his astuteness on many occasions, having witnessed his intellectual spars with some of the most impassioned speakers. Daulet was unequalled in an argument, so articulate was he. He could ridicule anyone. But this was not what the mighty Zhoneyut looked to his son for.

Now with the warlike strength of the tribe noticeably weakened, the last thing that the enemy needed to know was that there were internal quarrels. Zhoneyut and Daulet were the son and grandson of the great warrior Yer-Ogulan. If rumour got out across the steppe that the father had lost his authority over his youngest son, everyone would condemn the son and pour scorn on his father. Then Zhoneyut would lose all influence over his people.

This is why the father wanted to have a private talk to his son and heir; to find out as much as he could about this enigmatic figure, Daulet, who to all appearances was a great *dzhigit*. He wanted a confidential chat with him, to bring him to reason, once and for all.

The horses moved side by side, at a light trot, their paces in time with each other; the foxhounds scoured ahead, at times separating on the steppe and then joining up again; if one of them picked up a scent it would stop instantly, flattening its ears and sniffing the wind. Having lost the scent, the hound would return to the riders. Approaching midday, a herd of deer ran past and the dogs chased after them, their barks resounding amid the silence of the steppe. The hounds ran swiftly after the deer and soon disappeared. The riders did not pursue them, and the hounds were surprised when they did not hear the hunting horn behind them, and the pounding sound of horses' hooves. They ceased their chase. Exhausted and bewildered they settled down under some sparse *dzhida* bushes, and, panting heavily with lolling tongues and eyes half-shut, they waited for the riders to appear.

This day the riders showed no interest in hunting. Each kept a stubborn silence, their faces solemn. Zhoneyut, with fixed expression, looked away to the horizon. He sat stiff erect, high in his saddle and the only movement was from the sheepskin hat on his head, and the light flicker of his short whip. Daulet looked at his father from time to time and then, lowering his head, became absorbed in sombre thoughts.

The horsemen traversed the ridges scattered with stunted wormwood turning black from the heat, and came down from the hills onto a wasteland covered with a reddish crust of clay, scattered here and there with white sand-dunes. In front of them came crisp, cool air and Zhoneyut turned his horse. They rode on further still until the splash of water and the lapping of waves could be heard. The inland sea appeared suddenly from behind a hill. It stretched out to the horizon where it merged with the sky, conjuring shimmering mirages which so perturb the eyes and souls of weary travellers who have crossed the desert.

The waves crashed against the shore. When they rolled back baring the sandy bed, it seemed they handed the land back reluctantly. A cool breeze from the water ruffled the shoreline, and the waves rolled back and forth each overtaking the other like steppe grasses in the wind.

Zhoneyut turned his horse in the direction of a small peninsula: a sharp wedge of land protruding into the sea. A rocky ridge marked the beginning of the peninsula, and at its summit stood an ancient grave with a tombstone: with a tall column of dark, almost black, stone jutting out. Such tombstones are usually placed at the graves of the venerated. Time had smoothed the surface of the stone. The riders dismounted in front of the shrine and led their horses forward.

A flat boulder was rooted into the earth: this had been the sacrificial stone on which the pilgrims had lit a fire for the sacred cremation. The narrow wedge of the obelisk was strewn with cloths which had become faded by the sun. They were offerings to the dead given by those coming to pray at this sacred place. Bare bones lay scattered around, and the skulls of sheep and Arkhar ram horns had been thrown onto a pile: vestiges of pilgrims and hunters who had chanced by, and of travellers stopping here to pray.

Sinking to his knees, Zhoneyut began to recite a prayer in a hushed tone. Beside him, Daulet began praying, holding his palms in front of his face. The father lifted his arms up to the sky, then ran his upturned palms down his face from brow to chin. He finished off the ritual by wiping his forked beard. Whispering inaudibly the warrior Zhoneyut lightly sprang to his feet. Then it was Daulet's turn to complete the ceremony.

The old soldier tore down the rags tied to the obelisk without examining them, and hid them under his clothes: circus trappings should not disturb the dead. Then both father and son returned to their horses, untied them and led them away. When they reached the top of the stone ridge, with the horses still on a rein, a sharp gust of wind disturbed the manes of the horses and the hems of the *chapakh* coats flapped at the men's legs.

Still old Zhoneyut had not said one word to his son. He had deliberately brought Daulet to the ancient grave of Temirbaba. We have heard tales of the wisdom and spiritual strength of this holy ascetic. In days gone by, the most wise Shopan-ata was walking from Khorezm when he met Temirbaba here. At that time, the sea used to come right up to the stone ridge. The ascetic was sitting on the stone, cooling his feet in the water, and although it was a long way off, he heard someone coming in his direction. At last, whoever it was reared and stopped behind him. Temirbaba did not stir, nor did he turn to look at the traveller, who politely greeted him, bowing to the frail ascetic. But the holy man gave no reply. Shopan-ata was forced to introduce himself, revealing his name: famous among the inhabitants of the steppe. But Temirbaba maintained his silence, gazing out over the sea. The miracle maker Shopan-ata, in order that the ascetic might be aware of who was standing before him, said: 'You are great indeed, which is why you are so proud. However, let us have a contest.'

Only then did Temirbaba turn to him.

'Well then, you begin,' said the old man tersely.

'Very well,' replied Shopan-ata. 'Take a look over there. Do you see where the mountain goats are?'

'How could I not see them? Of course I see them.'

Shopan-ata started to mutter an invocation under his breath: 'Shorei, shorei, shorei.'

A large goat – a magnificent animal, a king among the Astrakhan breed, with great curved horns and a beard – came running down the steep decline towards the men. The animal, bleating, threw itself at Shopan-ata's feet, then lay on the ground and began to lick the hem of his robe. Then the miracle maker killed the goat and skinned it; slashed open its stomach and removed the entrails, then promptly and skilfully cut up the carcass with his bare hands. Having done this, Shopan-ata gave the frail ascetic a cheerful glance: then, without the least effort, he swiftly returned the carcass to its original form, putting back the entrails, stretching the skin back over the goat, and stroking its fur. Next, he blew and spat, and, lo and behold! the goat was the same as before. Then up it jumped and ran back to its herd.

It was now the turn of Temirbaba to display his sorcery. He raised himself calmly from the stone, rolled up his trousers to the knees and waded into the water. Further and further he waded but still the level of the water remained at his knees. The waves broke around him, the sea rose and rolled around him, and only the narrow ridge forming a new submarine followed the feeble ascetic forming a new peninsula. On seeing this Shopan-ata tore his white turban from his head and, waving it, called out: 'Stop! Come back! You are the more mighty! For the sake of Allah, stop!'

Only then did Temirbaba, having by now gone a long way out, stop where he was and turn. Shopan-ata called out, 'I was afraid that you would pass to the other side of the sea where our enemies would be able to reach us by this shortcut on the peninsula. Stop where you are and come back! You have convinced me of your great power!'

This is how that narrow promontory, like the blade of a dagger, was left as a relic of the meeting between the two great miracle makers. It is said Temirbaba ordered that he be buried at the very furthest tip of the promontory, at the top of the stony ridge.

'Come, all ye that are faithful,' said he on his deathbed. 'If you do not wish our ignoble enemies to come and relieve themselves on my grave, do not allow them to reach the sea.'

What more is there to say? The steppe is vast, its expanse boundless, but any foreign tribe may pass through it. The steppe cannot protect those that are weak. Look how the descendants of the Holy One will soon be unable to defend the sanctity of Temirbaba's grave. The stone which was placed as the foundation of the mausoleum was rough, but time and the elements have smoothed it. The obelisk is tall but half of it has now sunk into the earth, and only its narrow tip has been left protruding. Temirbaba's kinsmen to this day make for this place so as to draw strength from the sacred stones, covered in rust-coloured henna. There the soul of the great ascetic hovers. Those still alive remember his fortitude and return here time and again, to press their faces against the ancient stones covering the remains of the Holy One. Zhoneyut's grandfather, the *batyr* Ogulan, now long deceased, would come in mourning or in celebration; many times he took the young Zhoneyut with him. The old *batyr*'s eyes would light up when he surveyed his native lands, which could be seen from the summit where the Holy Temirbaba vigilantly guards the vast plains. If there had not been this holy guard, the nomadic tribes would have dispersed on their hardy Argamak horses, or lumbered along on the backs of their humped camels, scattering themselves among the barren valleys. Cut off from the water in the hills, by summer it is stripped to bare white sand. Dust storms have scattered the nomadic tribes along the steppe and all trace of them would disappear in the desert sands. The old *batyr* Ogulan used to say to his grandson, 'If it wasn't for this ancient tombstone, there would be nothing to remind us of the heritage of our ancestors; their renown, courage and steadfastness.'

From time to time, he would celebrate the brutality of his native tribe.

'We have no water but salt water from the sea. Nor do we have vegetation except for the stunted, prickly gorse. On one side we are surrounded by rocky mountains and on the other by sand. Such is our land and we have no other. But do not let anyone ever cast slurs on it. These sands and the sharp, rocky mountains are our protection and most reliable defence. If we had Iran's verdant terrain with its tropical gardens and fertile fields, where would we hide from our enemies?'

Such were the occasional utterances of the mighty Ogulan. However, neither the sands nor the mountain rocks could save his fellow tribesmen from being raided. It was the steppe cattle, the Argamak horses and rumours of treasures buried in chests by the desert-dwellers, which so attracted the enemy. Having had their fill of meat from the stolen cattle, the enemy turned its thoughts to seizing and expropriating the endless expanses which provide food for the many cattle. Then they lusted after the shapely Turkmen beauties, desiring to bed them.

Did these simple people who predict the weather by the belly of a horse, who presaged misfortune in the bark of the dogs – did they not know that the scheming enemy could creep up with a lasso in hand and throw it around their necks? Of course they knew, and lived in secret fear of it happening.

Zhoneyut reflected on this, standing on the shoreline and looking out to the sea. A strong wind ruffled the hem of his robe and moved the ends of his greying forked beard. In the distance the sea frothed with white foam as if it were sending muffled threats. The warrior Zhoneyut turned towards his son, and concealing his feelings no longer, took a long look at him. The father read in his son's eyes, luminous from suppressed worry, the answers to all the questions which he had not asked aloud. Daulet reverentially bowed his head before his father. Then Zhoneyut, his stern face rejoicing, seized the young man's arm and led him off to Temirbaba's tomb.

They fell silently to their knees and prayed, whereafter the young Daulet picked up a handful of earth and scattered it over the holy man's grave. They went to the tall obelisk and Daulet pressed his lips to it and felt the salty taste of the sea, breathing in the scent of it, carried by the winds of centuries and blended with the odour of the ancient earth and stone.

Still in silence the travellers moved from the holy shrine leading their horses behind them. At the bottom, Zhoneyut, having mounted his horse, again searched into the eyes of his son. Daulet did not look away: his eyes were full of peace, clarity and strength. Then the pilgrims returned to the *aul*.

In this way, without explanations or superfluous words, the legacy was passed on to the son. Peace and fulfilment reigned in the heart of the warrior Zhoneyut. Daulet had proved worthy of his great forefathers and had not disappointed his father, who was pleased his son possessed a heart which held dear the sacred traditions of the tribe. Zhoneyut made arrangements to send back to the stud Daulet's bay horse, which he usually rode when making visits and for general day-to-day purposes on the steppe such as searching for herds of horses.

The old warrior gave an order for a new fighting saddle to be brought out for everyone to see. According to the ancient rites of the tribe it was the duty of a young soldier, when going off on a military campaign, to leave on a grey piebald horse. So the herdsmen rounded up such a horse from the steppe, a five-year-old piebald stallion which had one distinguishing mark: a thick, coal-black strand in its tail which stood out noticeably amongst the grey. They penned up the stallion and began to break it in.

The elders of the whole *aul* gathered and began to inspect the stallion. It was agreed that the horse was an excellent one, strong and fit for battle. The black strand in the tail was noted which, according to superstition, was a sign of heaven's approval. The elders unanimously gave their blessing to the horse. It was Zhoneyut himself who saddled it up for the first campaign. The military saddle was brand new, hewn from the wood of a mature lime tree, with a high arch made especially to support the blunt end of a lance.

Daulet appeared, his long, curved sabre tied to his belt and a gun over his shoulder. He rode up swiftly on the new horse, impatient beneath him. Surrounding him, all the *dzhigits* let out a guttural cry, wishing him luck; and the women, confined to their homes and deprived of their menfolk, twitched the curtains of the entrance to the yurts so to gaze at the the broad-shouldered, handsome *dzhigit*. Even the old women were stirred, gazing at him with tears in their eyes remembering sons and husbands who had left long ago and were now lying in graves in foreign lands. As for the girls and young widows, they too shed a few tears in secret, having good reason.

Accompanying Daulet part of the way on his first campaign, Zhoneyut was visibly anxious. He pulled at his beard with wiry fingers. He still harboured grave doubts about Daulet even though he was good in armed combat, could hold a knife well, and was an excellent marksman. Yet, when it came to riding full speed at an enemy with a spear, having raised the heavy lance at his opponent, Daulet would forget to press the pikestaff into the saddle, and instead would hold it between the horse's ears aiming to thrust the spear at his opponent and knock him from the saddle. This however, would only succeed if the opponent was puny or slight. What if he were heavy and powerful? Also, while lancing, Daulet would try to rush headlong at an opponent instead of attacking from the side. But this was not all. Zhoneyut knew that his son avoided one-to-one combat. It was not that Daulet would lose composure or that his courage would fail. No, worse! He would hold back out of pity. And no matter how often the father showed his son how to fight effectively

– when to thrust the spear riding at full speed, or to dart to one side; when to tilt at the opponent with a battering ram with the aim of throwing him down to the ground – nothing seemed to result from the training he had been given. Daulet had neither the application nor the passion for fighting; he was not interested in military prowess like the warrior's other sons who had died young. At times, Daulet would fall into a reverie, becoming quite withdrawn, as if trying to remember something long lost, precious, and all but forgotten.

Chapter IV

It happened not long afterwards that Zhoneyut, on returning from a neighbouring village and riding up to the yurt, heard the sounds of a *dutar* coming from the yurt. It was unusual for people in his house to gather for amusement and merrymaking for they lived in trepidation of the stern warrior. But now, almost everyone who had remained behind in the *aul* had gathered round to sit in the shade behind the yurt, settling down together there. Even the women with wooden ladles boiling up sheep's cheese in the cauldron forgot to stir it, half closing their eyes in reverie, standing by the fire and wrapt in the music. Zhoneyut brought his horse to a stop and listened. The melody was sad, it reached to the very depths of his soul, and was full of nostalgia and overwhelming sorrow. A shudder went through Zhoneyut and he stood frozen to the spot, lowering his head to his chest. He had never experienced such a thing. His hair stood up on end from a sensation of fleeting sadness, as if he had received a fright. When Zhoneyut entered the yurt, Daulet, on seeing his father, stopped playing immediately, jumped to his feet, hung up his *dutar* on the wall and led his father to the place of honour. Zhoneyut said nothing to him.

However, three days later Daulet set off on his first campaign, heading the raid on the Adai *aul* of Dyuimkara. Zhoneyut's only surviving son was heading off to an unknown danger. The old warrior himself, along with several elders, accompanied the group of young braves part of the way, over five or six mountain passes.

The moment of parting had come. Giving his son a brief blessing, the warrior Zhoneyut turned his horse round and rode away. After a while he glanced back and could still make out the troop moving off in the distance. Travelling as a tight unit the riders looked like one body, their lances swinging above their heads, towering up towards the deep blue sky like a moving balustrade. The old warrior jerked his horse around and continued on his journey but after a little while stopped to take another look back: but the group of riders was out of sight hidden by the dense undergrowth bushes of the *garmala* which were shimmering in the haze. Oh steppe! You have devoured a handful of brave men! When Zhoneyut turned round for the third time, stopping on the top of the mountain pass, he could see only the empty horizon, the light blue expanse of the sky burned by the heat of the steppe below and shimmering in the delirium of the haze with its empty mirages.

A vague feeling of unease entered the old warrior's heart. He regretted not having gone with his son on the raid – it was his, after all, first martial campaign.

Having reached home, Zhoneyut was distressed and, addressing the elders, his old friends in combat, asked them to put off returning to their *auls* so that they might wait together for the *dzhigits* to return from the raid.

From that day on, the old warrior was never to have a true night's sleep. He would eternally await his son's return. He set up a guard on the watchtower of the burial mound so that he could not only warn of an enemy invasion but could also check from a distance for the return of the troop. From dawn until dusk the figure of the watchman was as a stake driven in to the earth, and through the lattice of the yurt Zhoneyut's long-sighted old eyes, narrowed in their observation of the watchman.

No one appeared from the direction of the mound, and in the stifling heat of the midday sun the only people to pass by were the four *mankurti*; victims of last year's revenge for the ignominious and terrible death of Zhoneyut's younger brother, Kekbor.

And then the long-awaited day came. From early morning the strange white light of the sunrise appeared like the yawn of a colossal beast. The morning passed, and once again the sky found its age-old blueness, washed-up to a shine. On the top of the pointed mound the figure of the vigilant watchman was in sight.

Zhoneyut shifted his clouded gaze from the watchman and solemnly regarded those seated around him. The elders lowered their heads. Many days had passed and still no news of the troop commissioned for the raid. Waiting for them to return was becoming much harder to bear. Then all at once a wiry Turkman who had been gazing at the empty steppe from under the half-opened felt entrance of his yurt, gave a start and turned to the west. At first, everyone turned to face him, then they too turned their heads in the same direction. From afar, they heard sounds, weak and indecipherable to begin with, then becoming louder and clearer.

Zhoneyut felt a wave of icy terror when he heard that cry. His legs went weak and although he made several attempts to stand he found he was unable to do so without help. People rushed out into the compound. Zhoneyut was the last to leave the yurt.

What are those dust clouds far off on the steppe? Not from the direction of the watchtower – not the watchman jumping up, his cry of joy resounding *'Siunshi! Siunshni!'* By tradition, whoever announces the victorious return of warriors from an incursion is due a gift: *'siunshi'*.

The first one to see the victorious troop returning home was indeed the watchman on the mound. But those advancing on horseback, kicking up the dust, were approaching from the wrong direction; and no, not crying out *'siunshi'*. It was a small group of riders. The piebald stallion was not amongst them. On the tip of a lone outrider's lance there fluttered a piece of white cloth: a sign of misfortune. The horses' hooves were kicking up a thick cloud of dust. Terrible wails of grief and horror could be heard:

'Oh, oh! *Baurim*. Brother! Oh, oh! What a tragedy!'

A chorus of lament rang out over the steppe. The riders, turning round in circles on the foaming horses, rocked backwards and forwards. It seemed as if the *dzhigits* no longer had strength to hold up the weight of their sheepskin hats.

The mournful cries of the grieving horde grew louder. What did all this mean? Zhoneyut froze, neither hearing nor seeing anything. The elders who had been standing around him began to beat themselves about the chest with their whip handles. Zhoneyut looked on them with anger and disgust, paying no heed to their wails. The men were now beating themselves about the head with clenched fists, while the women let out shrill cries, shaking and jerking under their black *yashmaks* like fish caught in a net. Why are they wailing and raving, scratching at their faces with their nails? Then they all turned in the direction of the yurt where the old leader's wife lived.

Old Anadurdy stood apart, sobbing and pulling at his beard. The tethered horses pawed at the ground, whinnying as if they, too, were sobbing. They bit at the tethering statues. The dogs yelped distractedly. The crowd involuntarily moved off, making for the steppe.

Only the *mankhurti*, dim-witted, dirty and dribbling, were oblivious to what was happening;

dragging their sacks to the pile of *kizyak* and throwing their loads to the ground, looking round vacantly.

One after the other, the riders appeared out of the cloud of dust and dismounted. Each one of them ran up to a stooping elder and threw himself to his knees, seizing hold of him and hiding his face. And the old men, with shaking hands, clutched each *dzhigit's* head in an embrace.

The terrible truth had dawned on Zhoneyut. He knew well enough why the people were rocking back and forth, hugging each other, sobbing on one another's shoulders. With knitted brows he scanned around as if in torment. Those around him, no longer in awe, cornered him on all sides, and began to embrace him, hanging on his neck. First one grey elder, then another; soon everyone began embracing him and bathing him with tears. Zhoneyut could hardly keep on his feet.

All of a sudden, from over someone's shoulders, Zhoneyut saw the piebald stallion standing alone, tethered to a post. Its tail had been cut off right to the rump. Five or so *dzhigits* dragged something into his yurt; something long and heavy, wrapped in a felt cloth. Behind them the crowd moved slowly in the settling dust. Two beardless elders, holding him by the arm, led Zhoneyut over to the yurt. He disengaged himself and stepped inside.

There, in the middle of the tent, lay the thing wrapped in a dusty, white felt rag. Those who had gathered round it began to bow before it and then, hurriedly, left the home in tears and more men were flocking into the yurt, wailing and lamenting:

'Oh, *baurim*! Oh, the young lad!' They, too, were looking at the felt wrapping, covered in thick dust and spattered with lumps of dried dirt.

Without warning, Mambetpana burst into the yurt, followed by Degen-akhun. Having barely crossed the threshold, the *bai* began howling, beating his chest; he embraced Zhoneyut. The mullah knelt down before the heap lying in the dust and started to murmur in a hushed voice. He raised his head and looked in silence at those standing round in the yurt, whereat they all began to leave, one after the other. Only the greybeards remained in the yurt. Degen-akhun went over to Zhoneyut. He stood by his right shoulder and began to mumble, mouthing under his thin moustache. Bewildered, Zhoneyut looked closer at the mullah's moving lips and long yellow teeth, but understood not one word.

Without waiting for a response, Degen-akhun turned towards old Anadurdy and summoned him over. Anadurdy came up, snivelling like a child, his beard damp with tears; he heard out the mullah and, not having the will to reply, could only nod his head. Several now stood up and formed a tight circle around the object lying in the middle of the yurt. Zhoneyut was led to Anadurdy's house; he sat in the place of honour beside his host, in complete silence, as if in a dream, who knows how long. At length an elder entered the yurt, leant down towards the host and whispered something in his ear, shaking his grey beard. The evening sun filtered into the yurt. All those present stood up, and Zhoneyut was taken by the arm and led away. Outside the yurt Degen-akhun stood waiting. He pointed in the direction of the setting sun and said something. Several *dzhigits* hurried towards Zhoneyut's yurt and dragged out the object, now tightly swaddled in a black felt cloth. The two *dzhigits* heaved it up on their shoulders and carried it out of the *aul* towards the burial mound. Several elders led Zhoneyut by the arm while he shuffled along obediently, utterly spent.

The long file of folk made off for the hill. The dust swirled up above the track. Breathing heavily and covered in sweat, the elders accompanying Zhoneyut struggled not to lag behind the hurrying crowd. Two *dzhigits* ran ahead and overtook the throng, catching up with the others who were carrying the black burden, and moving it over onto their own shoulders.

On the order of the mullah, a dozen or so men ran on, pushing through the scrubs to reach the higher ground. Having pulled out their swords, they began to cut down the bushes, only the clanking of their steel blades could be heard in the evening air. When the space had been cleared, they dug a hole. Beside it they heaped up a large pile of dry twigs. They placed on one side the rolled-up bundle and began to unwrap it, as it lay pale in the twilight. All those present fell to their knees in prayer. One of the *dzhigits* struck a flint to light a flame. The tinder started to smoke, and soon the pile of twigs leapt into flames. The wind had stilled, and only the plaintive voice of the mullah reading the words of a prayer resounded above with the crackling of the faggots.

The warrior Zhoneyut's soul was heavy. Everything around him was spinning as if in a nightmare. At last, he shook his head, opened his eyes wide and tried to rouse himself. But the nightmare had not passed. The throng seemed to be dispersing frenziedly. Was the enemy at hand? What had happened to them? Maybe a fierce enemy was nearby? If so, why were the Turkmen not mounted with their weapons in their hands, instead of running around causing a commotion?

Turkmen, where are your horses for fighting? What of your leader, the *batyr* Zhoneyut, son of the great Ogulan? Why was Zhoneyut being led off somewhere by two decrepit old men? Had the *batyr* made a grievous error, allowing the scheming enemy to triumph? What had become of his *aul*? Where were his children, his wives? Where was his son Daulet, his last remaining hope? Or had he too joined this shameful riot running from the enemy?

'Oh my little son, dear Daulet, why are you not with your father at this hour?'

Chapter V

Autumn had arrived and could be seen in the golden brown hues, and in the pale yellow patterns in the bright frills of the leaves of the trees and branches. There had been no rain during the summer. Even the hardy gorse had long since burned under the merciless sun. The woollen felt on the yurts was bleached and scorched, and had begun to break up; everywhere reeked of scorched wool. A languid mood dominated the *aul*. In the daytime not a soul was to be seen on the thoroughfare; everyone had retreated into their houses. It was long after midday, when the oppressive heat and closeness had eased, before people began to emerge. The women, on the orders of their husbands, would spread out their carpets in the shade and make up beds so that the men could come out to rest in the cool air. A short while later, they would call over their children and send one of them back to the house to fetch father's *papakha*. It is well known that a Turkman, when at home, wears a skull cap pulled over his shaven pate, but outside always adds to it the sheepskin *papakha*. The Turkman will pull the *papakha* over his eyes, recline in the sun, and as the hour approaches evening prayers, watch the shadows lengthen. Then he will take off the huge hat and begin to stroke it lovingly, running his fingers through the fur and examining it for moths. Beside each yurt there is a hatstand stake for the Turkman *dzhigit* to beat his *papakha* with a thin cane zealously, with a gleam of contentment.

After such energetic beating, the *dzhigit* again starts stroking and brushing the fur on the *papakha* with his fingers. Then he leaves it on the stake to air. At sundown he sends a boy to fetch the horses and saddles it up. The Akhaltekinets-Argamak horses, sleek and narrow-chested, fiery and tireless are not easy to saddle up. But when the horse is ready, the rider directs it towards the stake where the *papakha* is hanging. He does not put it on immediately, however. First, he despatches a boy to bring some water in a *kesushka*, then carefully sprinkles the fur. Then he twists the hat on his thumb, and twirls it fastidiously to arrange it on his head.

He swings into the saddle nimbly, barely touching the stirrups, and the Argamak under him is eager to be off, but the owner reins in, and circling on the spot scans around. Only then does he take off at a gallop to the steppe. Riders from neighbouring yurts also come galloping out of their compounds, all riding off in different directions on some business or other. The dust extends behind each rider. On and from the high knoll where the *aul* is situated the threads of dust resemble the yarn of a loom, torn this way and that.

This summer turned out to be a very dry one and soon there was nothing left for the animals to graze near the *aul*. The camels began to go far in search of fodder. Even the *mankurti*, whose heads had been compressed by the vice of the dried pelts which had become as hard as stone, stripping them of all human likeness – even they had lost sight of the camels despite trying to follow after them. The young camels, having lagged behind the adults, made pitiful noises and scampered across the steppe calling their mothers.

Now the sun is setting and twilight begins to encroach. The moon rises, filling the sky with milky light: darkness settles over the *aul*. The camels return in the cool evening air, their humps swaying, and horses too. The lowing of the corralled cattle and the cries of their owners break the quiet. On the road a cloud of dust has appeared, with towering silhouettes of camels or a rider on an Argamak horse, whose damp sides and rump gleam with sweat: limpid night figures approaching the *aul* from all directions.

And so one more day passes in the life of the *aul*, and soon all would settle down and go quiet. Only on the very edge of the *aul,* in a squalid shack with a leaking roof, a lone prisoner sits languishing with iron shackles on his wrists and ankles. For forty days and nights he has been in captivity, with no visitors, no one breaking up the endless monotony of his loneliness, but he has had more than enough time to observe life in the *aul* through the hole in the wall of the shack. At first, the prisoner was guarded by two men, then just one. But today they have again appointed two. The prisoner knew that the *aul* was in mourning for those warriors killed in the last raid.

Back home, in the Kazakh *aul*, he had noticed that on days of mourning crying could be heard frequently; whereas here, for days on end, there would be this lugubrious, ominous silence. Crying was heard only on the first day, when they made haste to bury Daulet. According to local custom, the deceased must be offered to the ground on the very day that the body is brought home. This has to be done before sunset. If this is not done in time, then it is done by the light of bonfires, and by midnight. To leave the body unburied until the next morning is considered a great sin. The Turkmen made haste to the cemetery and back almost at a run. A night-time funeral banquet had been arranged, and all those at the burial were to be served with dishes of stewed meat. But on the night of the funeral, it looked like no one would touch the funeral food and everyone hastily departed before sunrise. The meat was left for the dogs to eat. From that day forth, the *aul* had fallen into an ominous silence, like a long, dismal dream.

And so it was that forty days passed. The piebald stallion, whose tail had been lopped off at the rump, was tethered to the large, dark yurt. Until now he had grazed with the herd in order to be fattened up. Now he had been brought back. Some Turkmen went over to the horse and conversed among themselves, shaking their *papakhas*. Then they untied the stallion and led him off by the reins.

'Where have they taken the stump-tailed horse?' the prisoner asked one of the guards.

'They are going to slaughter it. Today marks the forthieth day since Daulet was killed.'

'Oh, so that's why.'

It was not for nothing that so many visitors appeared in the normally deserted *aul*. By the large, dark yurt, where for the last forty days not a soul had been seen, many saddled horses were tethered. The prisoner had not seen the owner of the yurt in the last forty days: the warrior had not left his yurt in all this while. The visitors, mainly grey-bearded elders, did not spend long inside Zhoneyut's home; having entered, they soon made their way out again and hastily untied their horses. At night, when all were asleep in the *aul*, the guards would converse with the prisoner and tell him many things. The prisoner found out that Zhoneyut had not spoken in forty days; that at first he had not been able to grasp that his son had been killed and been buried, and that it was after a rout that the troop returned. He had given an order for the guard on the mound to remain for another week. The most respected elders from various Turkmen tribes visited, attempting to offer Zhoneyut comfort and to make him see reason. But Zhoneyut continued to keep his silence, sitting like one who had been turned to stone. He would sometimes pull at his half-white beard. Then, however, Anadurdy and some elders went in to remind him that the forty day anniversary of Daulet's death was almost upon them.

In this way, the prisoner discovered exactly how long he had been under arrest. It was forty-two days ago exactly when he set off to hunt Arkhary rams and shortly afterwards was taken prisoner. Hunting always distracted him from the commotion of festivities and banquets he was obliged to attend. The prisoner was a well-known *dombra* player, a *Kiuishi*, and his art was cause for his being always in company. Yet, since he was a child, he had always preferred solitude, seclusion, and quiet meditation. His great fame had stopped him from living as he would have liked since he was constantly being persuaded to take part in lavish celebrations and all types of musical contests, where it was hard to find his match. All the same, this *Kiuishi* preferred solitude to the noisy life of performing for others.

He could not endure what he saw going on around him. Living in an *aul* was a constant source of worry because of its close proximity to enemy tribes; one day there would be a noisy celebration, the next, crying and wailing would be heard due to some bereavement: there was no peace for the naturally solitudinous man. If two young rascals came to fisticuffs over a game of dice, their fathers, all fired up would go for each other with daggers. Oh, Allah! Fighting over such trifles, their faces contorted with rage, murder in their eyes and teeth grinding. And the very reason for starting the ignominious brawl long forgotten! Beaten black and blue with gaping wounds on their bodies, both would fall to the ground, where they belong, where they both rot.

Where contests and duels take place, there you will find bones mixed up with broken fragments of spears and daggers, horse dung and jackal excrement. In time, all of this breaks down into the earth and is reduced to dust. How to tell one *batyr*'s remains from another's? Who had an honourable death, and who a disreputable one? Where are their fearless, fervent hearts now? They have been eaten by worms and by flies in some unmarked burial mound. Each will leave behind orphan sons, to grow into men bearing savage hatred for each other without ever having met: who will spend their lives trying to avenge the death of their illustrious fathers. With barely a whisker on their face, they will set off on an incursion with the friends of their dead fathers in order to avenge the death of their forebears.

It is the same with the enemy, since the enemy's children will also grow up lusting after revenge; unassuageable revenge. This is how people will live from one generation to another, from century to century; rivers of blood will be spilt in the process. But the earth is indifferent to all this. Let them spill as much blood as they like: the earth will receive everybody, both those puffed up with arrogance and pride, and the poor and meek; the earth has room for them all. People may count their victories but they will never defeat the earth for she is their eternal refuge. She will wait her turn patiently and then take what is hers. There is always a place under the earth for those who feel restricted in life.

Why are they so restless? They rush around causing a commotion, and disturb their great ancestors, invoking their names. Another poor soul scrabbles around unable to feed either himself or his family even by honest labour, but muddles around here and there, muttering about some sacred duty to the souls of his forefathers. He displays great zeal for performing his duty to the dead, but will himself soon end up dead. Is there really so little space for them on this earth? Will they not rest until they have killed one another? At the most abundant time of year, when the steppe and the hills are filled with joy and love, they desert their wives and children, abandon all the things they have acquired over the years; leave behind their cattle and give up the peaceful life of herdsmen to set off on an incursion in order to plunder, rape and commit murder in foreign lands. Then, having achieved what they set out to do and having had their fill, they return home in victorious triumph. Thereafter, sitting at home, they listen out for any sound that may signal retribution from the enemy. For the victors – predators and bloodsuckers, rapists and plunderers during the hostilities – there will be no peace of mind.

When the next war with all its excesses seems a long time off, the steppe fighters begin to yawn with boredom; for the sake of amusement they set animals on each other, even if it is a goat with a dog. If his hands are still itchy and he cannot keep boredom at bay, then the fighter will go off and pick an argument about some foolish matter with his neighbour so there is often cause for minor quarrels, fights, squabbles, rivalry, theft and murder. Why is it, steppe-dweller, that you are incapable of living a peaceful existence? Or will you only rest in the grave? You will be put in the ground quickly and then those who yesterday goaded you to set upon imaginary enemies, they will be the ones to start wailing, beating themselves about the head with their fists, and tearing at their hair: they will mourn the deceased as befits tradition.

But let the hypocrites sob; let their crocodile tears fall! Let the dark blood gush at last from their eyes! He who sheds tears for the deceased today and tomorrow goes off to kill, he too is sure to be killed sooner or later. Indeed, the dead bury the dead!

Man is like an animal. Until he feels pain he does not think of the suffering of others. It is only when grief and suffering have touched him personally does he see things more clearly; only when he has shed tears that he begins to grasp the realities of life.

So the prisoner reflected while he sat in captivity. What do we reflect on as we sit in the captivity of life? Do our thoughts differ fundamentally from those of the prisoner? He sits languishing in captivity, peering through the holes in the wall of that hovel. Today he saw the tethered piebald stallion led to slaughter and saw the *aul*, which had been desolate for forty days, come back to life. They were getting ready for the feast in memory of the dead warrior.

The prisoner felt his strength sapping away; felt his heart hardening like a crushing weight in his chest. Sleep evaded him. His soul was becoming black from all his sombre thoughts and the blood pounded in his temples; he was beginning to lose all hope of salvation.

The prisoner's face was pale and emaciated, his hands shook in the fetters, and either he was chilled to the bone or covered in sweat. He had fallen ill, for the forty days of unbearable captivity had brought him to the brink of death. He sensed death was already close, and without even understanding himself what it was that he was seeking, what he missed most of all, he started to rummage about in front of him with both hands. Later the prisoner returned to his senses and realised that he was searching for his *dombra*, his friend in hour of need, to whom he had been used to revealing all the mournful secrets of his soul.

In a weak voice he asked the guards about something, but they moved off, and with a glance over to Zhoneyut's yurt, began to count the number of horses tethered to the posts. Losing all hope the prisoner fell silent lowering his head to his chest and shutting his eyes. He stirred when someone pulled at the sleeve of his *chapan*. When he raised his head, the prisoner saw standing before him a familiar face, that of the old man Anadurdy, the Turkman fortune-teller and *dutar* player. They had met in musical contests during the years of the great reconciliation in the territory of the Adai, the Turkmen's nearest neighbours. Anadurdy said a few words to the guards and they replied, but the prisoner did not take anything in. At last they told him to get up and leave the prison along with the guards and the old man, Anadurdy.

And so it was that, a short time later, he found himself inside the large, dark yurt of the warrior, Zhoneyut. Such was the silence inside that the prisoner thought that it was empty and wondered why he had been brought there. When he looked around, however, he saw that there were indeed people inside, elders, and all were sitting in total silence facing the *tor*. From here the figure of an old man rose like a carved image, his hair as white as hoar frost and his long beard, which hung from his sunken cheeks, parted in two. A shudder went through the prisoner when he realised that it was the *batyr* Zhoneyut, the father of the slain Daulet, who held the frail thread of his fate in his hands.

Chapter VI

During the forty day mourning period, Zhoneyut the warrior was not once left alone. It seemed as if the *batyr* neither saw nor heard anything; he uttered not a single word, nor replied when spoken to. Today however, it was as if he had woken from a deep sleep, and for the first time he took a careful look around him. Grave was the look of the warrior whose hair had turned from grey to snow-white, and when the prisoner was led in and placed in front of him, the warrior stared at him with consternation. In front of the *batyr* Zhoneyut the pitiful figure looked barely alive: pale and emaciated, he was a shadow of his former self. The prisoner, in his dirty, torn clothes and iron fetters, provoked a feeling of loathing in the old warrior.

The Kazakh prisoner was almost bent double with exhaustion as he paused by the entrance, hands hanging to his knees. He did not look around but stared through swollen eyelids at the wall opposite, as if nothing was of any interest to him. One might suppose he was proud and fearless, that he was indifferent to his own fate and to all those around whose eyes were fixed upon him. Yet anyone taking a closer look at the prisoner could hardly suspect him of arrogance. It was obvious that the man was wasting away and could barely remain standing.

He was ordered to come forward and stand nearer to the *tor*, the place of honour, but as he did not catch their words, one of the men with white beards jumped up and seized the prisoner by his fettered hands, guiding him to the middle of the yurt. The prisoner could barely walk. The man with the white beard removed the handcuffs, and took a step back. The prisoner, impassive to all that was going on around him, remained rooted to the spot.

Zhoneyut, with an angry glance, took in the rows of *papakhas* around him. 'What is this? Are you offering this as recompense for my murdered son?' he seemed to say. 'For my son this half-dead *kiuishi*?' At this, the sheepskin *papakhas* bowed before him. Only one head did not bow, that of Anadurdy who fixed his furious glare on the old man and rose up silently to slink out of the yurt. Once more Zhoneyut turned his attention to the pitiful prisoner, who continued to stare impassively at the lattice of the yurt. Zhoneyut could have killed him with a glance. On the witless face there was not a trace of fear, nor any sign of a soldier's pride. Lanky, his long arms dangling, only his protruding Adam's apple moved up and down.

The old man, Anadurdy, returned to the yurt. He went over to the prisoner and held out an oblong, wrapped in a grey cloth. It took the prisoner a while to grasp what was that was required of him. Lowering his eyes, he peered at the object, and all at once his face flushed. It was clear he wanted to say something but his lips moved wordlessly. He held out his hands awkwardly, and with a timid look accepted what was being offered. Having taken hold of the long bundle, the prisoner sat down jerkily, his legs buckling beneath him. Only now did he take in those gathered around him. His expression of joy flared up in his eyes. With trembling hands he removed the grey cloth, and on his knees there lay a *dombra*; his old *dombra*, with the elegant marquetry on the sounding board. He looked down upon the instrument in silence and then, taking it up, began carefully to turn the pegs. All those present in the yurt watched him, holding their breath.

Anadurdy stealthily picked his way back to his former spot and sat. The two guards who had come in with the prisoner squatted down by the yurt's entrance. In the ensuing quiet, sounds of the *dzhigits* talking loudly outside could be heard as they cut up the sacrificial horse, and the sounds of dogs growling as they came running up, attracted by the smell of blood.

Shafts of weak autumn sunlight came through the opening of the yurt, cutting through the semi-darkness, revealing Zhoneyut's face, broad shoulders and powerful straight-backed figure.

The prisoner still showed no interest in those present, seemingly oblivious of the warrior Zhoneyut looming over him ominously. The prisoner's hands, chafed by fetters, had become clumsy; his swollen fingers ran over the finger board making strange sounds, tripping on each melody. The *dombra* had been exposed to heat which had affected its sound, and the pegs had weakened and would not hold the strings at an appropriate tension, making it impossible to tune the instrument.

How can we expect a *dombra* to have a good sound if, forty-two days previously, it too, was taken captive and had since been parted from its maker? It was when he had left Kok-baur to go hunting for Arkhari rams that he had been overtaken by a troop of Turkmen riders not far from the foothills. As a man they had raised a loud war cry over the steppe. He had stood calmly where he was with his gun hanging over his shoulder. He had not harmed anyone and had only set out to hunt. But among those in the troop were some of the Turkmen who had accompanied Daulet on his visit to the Adai and had seen the prisoner during the famous music contest. They were the ones who shouted the loudest, addressing the leader. One in particular stood out, with a hooked nose and spittle issuing from his mouth, who tried to demonstrate something by pointing at the *dombra*. Then, two of them rode over to him and seized his gun and *dombra*. Only then did he first feel alarmed. He thought that he would never again see his *dombra*; but now he saw it once more and held it in his hands.

Zhoneyut, his hair white hoar frost, gave a sombre glance at the pitiful prisoner. The latter returned the warrior's stare, then hung his head over his *dombra,* his expression serene like a mother observing her child suckling at the breast.

Zhoneyut followed the prisoner's every movement like a hungry predator scrutinising his victim. Could he really be thinking of playing more? No, he could not possibly with his distorted hands like the curved twigs of a *saksaul*; he must simply be examining his dried-out piece of wood, handling it, stroking it, glad he had it back again. He was trembling with joy, unaware of anything going on around him. 'And to think that this worthless creature, this numbskull, was taken as hostage by my *batyri* in exchange for my beloved, murdered Daulet!' thought Zhoneyut. Would any person in their right mind really go out alone onto the steppe, where a merciless war of vengeance rages? To take such a person hostage does not require great valour, yet his was the one life offered in exchange for Daulet.

The old warrior turned his back on the prisoner, and his eyes flashed at those around him. These elders, respected people and well-known fighters in their tribes, could not hold his stare and hung their heads.

In the meantime, the prisoner continued to strum and pluck the *dombra*, trying to tune it; he adjusted the strings and turned the pegs, lowering and twisting his head to one side as he did so, listening out for the sounds. The Turkmen, sitting patiently on the rugs, began to sweat from beneath their *papakhas*, beads of moisture dropping from forehead and temples. They were silent, and all were looking at Zhoneyut. He too was silent, and in that silence there was something ominous.

In the hands of the musician the *dombra* gradually came to life, its sound becoming deeper, taking on a more resonant, singing sound. At last, the first strains of a tune spilled forth and, though short, hesitant and faint, it nevertheless began to sound like music. Soon the sounds of the music grew stronger, and finally it rang out in resonant tones. In a clear voice, the *dombra* spoke of pain, yearning, grievances, loss, love; of the irrevocability of happiness: all the aspects of the life of a prisoner whose days and nights are spent in endless solitude. The mellifluous sound stunned the listeners.

The formidable old man with the stern face and snow-white beard that hung from cheeks furrowed with wrinkles, stared at the *dombra* player with shining eyes. He had spent many days in tomb-like silence as if he had been buried alive, nursing the sorrow that had burned a hole in his soul. Even though he had been surrounded by many helpers, elders and guests who had come from afar, Zhoneyut had sat fixed to his spot and not spoken a word, as if he did not see them. A person is always alone in his grief; infinite grief cannot be shared, and the person will feel alone even when surrounded by people.

But now the warrior Zhoneyut, as if awoken by the music stealing up on a soul frozen these forty days and nights, straightened up and looked at his tribesmen anew. He wanted to show them that he was resolute and strong, and that the great pain in his soul, the heartache had passed. He was calm and collected once more, and ready to lead an army off on an incursion.

Zhoneyut once more gathered his strength. He knitted his brows, no longer wishing to reveal weakness. He had the impression that his people were waiting for him to rouse himself, and to inspire them all by giving out a cry; saddling the war-horses, and setting off on an incursion so as to avenge the enemy in a fitting manner.

Meanwhile, the *Kiuishi* decided to let his playing express for him all the awful suffering and pain that he had undergone while he had been in captivity, and to pour into his music the anger and resentment of an innocent man who has been tormented. A sudden thought came to the *Kiuishi*: 'What did all this matter to an ignorant, bloodthirsty warrior?' It became clear to him that his efforts would be in vain. 'Who was there to appeal to and why? The grey-haired *batyr* would hear him and then jeer and curl his lip in derision. After this, he would order his curs to slice him into small pieces with their sabres. No, it would be better not to continue with this *kiuiy*.'

The musician sharply struck the string with his middle finger and stopped playing. The yurt fell silent. And then, the prisoner began to play a completely different tune, not aggressive and angry like the first one, but a quiet song, giving vent to sadness. His deformed fingers like the crooked branches of the *saksaul* seemed to have taken on a new life, and ran across the body of the *dombra,* gracefully plucking at the strings. The prisoner started up a new *kiuiy,* one that had come to him during those grim days and nights in captivity when his hands were in fetters and he had been deprived his *dombra.* At that time, he could only rummage around in the dark, his fettered hands searching for his instrument. And now, he had his *dombra* with him and for the first time his music, which had been composed and memorised in the darkness of the torture chamber, was being heard.

He sat comfortably, holding the instrument to one side, aloof, but with fire in his narrow eyes. No one could come between the *Kiuishi* and his music. These savage folk in their huge hats faded from him; the huge, white-haired old man with sombre, dark eyes had disappeared also. The only thing to be heard in the silence was the music, which seemed to come not from the old *dombra* but to have flown in from outside, from the far-off skies, from the wide, sprawling steppe.

Old Zhoneyut did not notice that he had fallen under the spell of the pervading music, composed by the pitiful prisoner who resembled a sick young kestrel or merlin. At first the warrior tried to resist the pull of the music, attempting to maintain his stern expression and knitting his heavy, thick brows; but as if under a powerful enchantment, he listened as the musician's fingers fluttered over the the *dombra*.

The poignant melody filled the yurt which seemed held under the spell of a dream. The music's charm had for this fleeting moment tamed the cruel world of the *aul*; these warring nomads in *papakhas* ranked around their chieftain, and this hoary warrior – for even he was enthralled by the musician – sat entranced by the music which for a moment became more convincing than the real world.

A new *kiuiy* struck up. Its tune was at first soothing, deep reflection and intelligent reasoning could be heard in its melody. For many years, the musician had longed to play this *kiuiy,* which flew from the depths of his heart; but he had restrained himself. He thought how in life evil and cruelty always got the upper hand, and how the tenderness of music could lament the overpowering of good by evil. And so it was that the virtuoso ended up in a Turkmen prison, sitting in a stinking hovel for a cell, his hands and feet bound in iron fetters, contemplating music that was more powerful than any ill deed. Once in the dead of night, he heard his composition clearly as if it were being played somewhere near to him.

How many times, incarcerated in the *zindan*, had he felt like picking up a *dombra* and playing that *kiuiy* for the last time. Now, with his old instrument in his hands, he could at last express all that he had buried in his heart for so long. He could reveal all to these old people, who in wars and raids had lost their dearest children, their support and hope in old age. He could offer comfort to this mighty warrior who had lost his last son. At that moment the *Kiuishi* felt powerful; he could rouse their hearts, soften the violence of the steppe predators and reveal to these cruel bellicose people their own soul which was full of tender humanity. And all this was thanks to having held, once more, his *dombra* in his hands.

Today, when they led him into Zhoneyut's yurt, the prisoner had noticed a *dutar* hanging on the lattice wall. This was a Turkmen instrument, related to the Kazakh *dombra,* and it was on seeing this that the musician became almost feverish. The idea that he would never again hold his old *dombra* was unthinkable. A miracle had occurred! He had got it back, and was now playing the very *kiuy* which had so tormented him in prison, coming to him at night and giving him no rest, so clearly did it sound in his ears against the deathly silence of the cell.

At first he had found it difficult to contain his excitement; his head spun, his legs buckled beneath him, and his hands trembled: just so a mother camel, having been separated from her young for several days, cannot give milk when she next sees her offspring, so overwhelmed is she that all her milk ducts close.

Now he is playing a *kiuy,* singing how sweet life is on earth, how magnificent in its glorious expanses. And why must they fight and kill each other, these brother nations, when it is so good to live out one's days in joyful labour: days watching the children grow, and seeing them prosper, days which reach wise old age.

Zhoneyut turned his gaze from the musician for an instant and noticed that his people had become transformed. Only a little while ago they had watched for any little change in his expression, not taking their eyes off him. Now here they were, all of them, mesmerised by the prisoner with the *dombra* in his hands. The eyes of the steppe-dwellers shone from underneath their *papakhas* with an unusually chastened expression. Gone was the warlike aggression in their looks, the age-old violence of the steppe fighters. None of this remained on their faces, which had been wiped clean by the purity of the music. It seemed to Zhoneyut that his aides, helpers and comrades-in-arms had forgotten about him, so enthralled were they by the emaciated prisoner. Incensed, Zhoneyut cast them a furious glance, yet for some reason it had no effect. No one even looked round. And then Zhoneyut remembered the words of his dead brother, Kekbor. He had said that all these *kiuishi-bakshi dutar* players were servants of dark forces, and that the *shaitan* helped them. Otherwise, how could they bewitch a whole throng and make them listen for hours on end? Yes, this is what Kekbor had said and now his older brother could see with his own eyes that it was true. The warrior had to admit that this half-dead *Kiuiyshi* had single-handedly overcome all his *dzhigits*, fellow fighters and comrades-in-arms. Zhoneyut the warrior could not pardon the musician such a thing. He had gained the upper hand over his, the *batyr* Zhoneyut's, military authority.

Oh, you all know this last *kiuiy* of the prisoner-musician. He sang of how people waste their lives if their only aim is to kill each other. What is it that they lack on this, God's earth? They are unable to take pleasure in the simple things in life, always desiring more; they rage with envy in their hearts and, until their greed has been sated, they will always feel confined whether at home or on the wide expanse of the steppe. The bones and skulls of their warring ancestors will never be a reliable shield to defend and screen the borders of their land from enemies. Man should try not to see in another man his enemy for then he would have no enemies. To become a man one must first know what suffering is. If you have never felt pity, how to do you expect anyone to pity you in your hour of grief and bitter loss? No one will. You will be all alone. If you set out with a sword to attack your enemy and you are killed, you will be alone for eternity. Do not curse God above or your enemy below, curse yourself. Do not rage and splutter like boiling water spilling from an urn; do not try to take revenge on anyone over your domain on this earth.

Better that you humble yourself. Make peace with yourself, for only then will you become a man. Master yourself, for only then will you become a man. If you try to sink your teeth into another, or claw at your enemy, how do you distinguish yourself from an animal? A ferocious beast does not expect pity from people. If you are killed then do not expect to be mourned, for people do not mourn animals. You alone will be the reason for your death and you alone will be to blame, and neither God nor your enemies on this earth will have anything to do with it.

Do you understand what I am talking about? Are you only listening to me so as to distract yourselves from this earthly boredom? If the sound of my music is pleasing to you, then maybe my ideas will sink into those heads of yours, hidden under your military *papakhas*. You are subdued and meek today, but tomorrow will you again set off on a raid? Most likely, yes; most likely you will and that grieves me. No, you do not have it in you to be men! Humanity is beyond you. Only through sorrow, unhappiness, misfortune and suffering can you glimpse your humanity; this alone will help you to become men. In sorrow you resemble men. But as for the rest, you are animals, and like them you forage around looking for prey.

When the *kiuiy* ended, unshed tears glistened in the eyes of the pitiful prisoner with his *dombra*. Not taking his eyes off him, Zhoneyut smiled darkly. He thought that the Kazakh, with his playing on the *dombra*, was trying to arouse his pity, trying to beg for mercy. The musician raised his eyes to the warrior. He looked at the mighty warrior with a searching expression, and in the gaze of the doomed prisoner there was neither entreaty, nor fear, neither reproach nor anger. His fingers flew over the strings, and the musician seemed to have recovered completely.

Towards the end, a chill was felt from the mournful music as if it were a dirge. The tune kept its pace but grew more quiet, and only once did it crescendo anew and falter wildly. Zhoneyut was reminded how on the eve of his son's incursion on the Adai, he had caught Daulet in the yurt playing on the *dutar*; the tune that he played had also caused a chill to come over him. But the stern *batyr* did not realise at the time what this heralded, thinking only that it was his old bones beginning to ache.

'What are they lamenting for, these *Kiuishi-bakhshi* and *dutar* players? What do they endlessly mourn for? What do they mean to tell us with tears in their eyes?' thought Zhoneyut, glancing across at the prisoner-musician. His gaze held neither fear, nor timidity. It was as if he wanted to divine the old soldier's every movement and Zhoneyut was the first to drop his gaze. He attempted to remain impassive, staring at the top cross-beam of the doorway, but his eyes could not hide his deep sorrow and great pain, and in them there suddenly flashed a blaze. It seemed that at that moment he had come to an irrevocable decision, and although the sorrow on his face was still visible, in his eyes there appeared a terrifying bitterness. The prisoner thought that the warrior was trying to muster his old feelings of enmity and summon up cruelty in his heart. Surely a person with such a sad face cannot be truly cruel? The prisoner-musician plucked at the strings once more, and the quiet strains of a new *kiuiy* resounded.

The tune was full of tender sadness and soft, comforting peace. The music caressed the audience, enveloping their grief-stricken hearts, for a moment, the memories of the good days conquered the heart of the old soldier, and in his mind's eye he could see his young sons standing before him. A tremor ran through Zhoneyut's body, and tears filled his eyes.

Oh, old warrior, where have your firmness and your fierce, unbending will gone? The music has bewitched you, and truly the power of the *shaitan* lurks in it. For forty days and nights after the death of his youngest son, Zhoneyut had sat in total silence and not shed a tear. This small wooden instrument, the *dombra,* could work such wonders! And this gaunt prisoner with his pale face, how did he manage to invoke in the old man's heart such pain for the irretrievable and irrevocable?

In his period of mourning the old warrior happened to look in the direction of the curved wall where, on the wooden latticed frame of the yurt, hung the dead Daulet's *dutar* beside his dagger and spear. When Zhoneyut's older sons had died, their spears and swords had been hung up: now all were dead, killed in raids, and only their weapons remained in their father's house as a reminder.

On the day that Daulet had mounted his piebald war-horse and the elders had given him their blessing for what he was about to do, Zhoneyut had brought him this spear. What had this weapon brought him? Fame? Luck? And his other sons who had died in foreign lands. What had it brought them, except an early death? 'Oh Daulet! my youngest son, your father's last hope! You are gone forever.'

Zhoneyut jumped up from where he sat and in a blind rage tore Daulet's dagger and spear from the wall. With two blows on the iron fender of the fire, he smashed them to pieces. He did not touch the *dutar*. From that day forth, it was as if everything in his soul had died; – and all that remained was anger, black hatred and a boundless hunger for revenge. He seemed like a wounded animal which, if merely touched, would set upon one in a ferocious frenzy. But even a wounded animal can be tamed with care and kindness; a person seized with anger and hatred, what can be used to calm him?

The melody poured forth, its rhythm swift and delightful. It seemed that the the musician himself was transported by the sound, and that in the eyes of his audience and tormenters the *Kiuishi* had been transformed. He had dreamed of such a moment. Now he could express everything that had lain in his heart like a deathly burden. To express all this without an angry cry, or humiliating tears, but in the quiet, measured language of music, filled him with wonder. The audience did not stir, nor utter a single sound.

Outside on the roadway, not a sound could be heard. The grey-bearded elders bowed their heads to their chests, and it might have seemed that the old men were dozing. But the *Kiuishi* could see that each of them was spellbound by his *kiuiy*. Even the two burly guards, sitting by the door and leaning on the handles of their horsewhips, were listening to the music with a pensive look upon their faces. In a separate group sat the warring *sarbazi* who had returned alive from the last incursion; not one of them looked either at their chieftain, Zhoneyut, or the *Kiuishi*. Each was going over his innermost thoughts while listening to the soft music.

Perhaps it reminded them of a lullaby which their mother had sung to them when they were small; or maybe they were recalling how their young wives, trying to hold back the sobs and tears, had seen them off on perilous incursions. The *dzhigits* tried with all their might to restrain themselves, but they were on the verge of tears. They hurried to cross the small path to the place where their battle-horses, the tethered Argamaks, were champing at the bit and pawing the ground. The *dzhigit*, having mounted his horse, would charge off in a cloud of dust. How their hearts would ache in their chests, as if they had been torn and clawed at by dogs. At such a point, the steppe fighter, in order to overcome momentary weakness, would try to kindle hatred for his enemy in his heart and would remind himself that vengeance on him was obligatory.

The steppe fighter would want to catch up with the enemy as soon as he could, overpower him and cut him into pieces. The *sarbaz* imagines how the despised enemy would fall with a crash to the ground along with his horse from the mighty blow dealt to him, and his dark blood would seethe as it flowed from the wound. This picture would soothe and satisfy the fighter's soul, and he would be happy as if he had caught up with the enemy and defeated him in battle.

Has it really never happened, *sarbaz*, that from your blow some young, inexperienced enemy soldier has fallen to the ground under his horse's feet? In the height of battle, with horses and men, zealously fighting to the death, you only have time to look for a second into the face of the man you have conquered as he flies past on his ferocious horse. But later, after the battle when you have time to yourself, you recall the face of your defeated enemy, still so young and inexperienced, and all of a sudden you feel remorse. You are disgusted with yourself and feel like a murderer. But you repress this, trying not to reveal your weakness; embittered, you summon up exultation at having accomplished the act of vengeance. This does not ring true. The truth is that you are a murderer. And now this *dombra* and this hushed *kiuiy* have opened up the hearts of these fighters to truth and sincerity: no, the *dombra* does not lie.

The *Kiuishi* continued to play, shifting his fixed and enigmatic gaze once more to Zhoneyut. Just like a shaman charming a snake, it seemed as if the music could reach the innermost depths of a man's heart. There began to appear in the music something sorrowful and insistent; something that drew the listener in; which amazed all those present and made them raise their eyes to look at the *Kiuishi*. He was not asking for mercy: he did not allow himself to be humiliated in front of those who had tormented him. He was simply performing on the *dombra* while they listened, tears filling their eyes and their hearts ready to burst.

It was affecting old Zhoneyut in the very same way. He looked at the emaciated *Kiuishi* in astonishment. He knew that very tune: Daulet had played it on the very eve of the fateful incursion. These *bakshi*, they possess inexplicable magic powers, and the dead Kekbor was right to have detested them. He had not been able to bear either music or women's tears, this mighty *batyr*; and whenever he came across a celebration where music was being played or entered a house where women were crying he would try, at first, to drive out all the musicians and silence the women. If this did not work, he would turn his horse round and ride off. Zhoneyut, likewise, had been uncompromising all his life, and neither listened to music nor approved of merrymaking. When this grave misfortune occurred and he lost his favourite son, the old warrior almost went mad with grief; but the resoluteness of his soul held out and over the forty days and nights he had not shed a single tear. But here, listening to this miserable *Kiuishi*, his people had been moved to tears. They sat placid, crestfallen, and many of the *sarbazi* also had tears in their eyes.

In the area of the yurt where all manner of utensils and junk had piled up, between two upper battens of the frame, a string had been pulled across on which had been threaded forty unleavened pancakes. They had been hung up on the day that the warrior's young son had died. Every day, Deneg-akhun had come and had taken down one pancake after the evening prayers and, having broken it up into little pieces, he would hand it round to the guests. Today, only one pancake remained on the string, and this evening it would be gone. Just as these forty pancakes had disappeared, so would the memory of the handsome *dzhigit*, beloved Daulet, gradually disappear.

The *kiuiy* finally came to an end. Silence reigned in the yurt. The *Kiuishi* prisoner dropped the *dombra* to his knees and slumped with exhaustion. The proud, old *batyr* wiped his eyes and face with his hands; his grey whiskers and forked beard, which hung down from his sunken cheeks, were damp with tears.

The prisoner sat in front of him looking crestfallen; his forehead covered in sweat which he did not bother to wipe away. Looking directly in front of him with unblinking eyes, the *Kiuishi* silently awaited his fate.

He was clearly tired: his eyes kept shutting and it was with effort that he would open them again. The Turkmen sitting around them stirred as if they were awakening with difficulty from the spell of the music.

Zhoneyut, the old warrior, chieftain of the tribe, sat looking unwaveringly at the prisoner. Then he shifted his gaze away and turned back to the elders. The latter began to stir and their *papakhas* shook. Zhoneyut straightened his back decisively and signalled with his hand to the two guards who had fetched the Kazakh prisoner from his cell. The bearded guards jumped to their feet and moved to the prisoner, once again putting fetters on him. Holding him by the arms, they dragged him to the exit. The people in the yurt, holding their breath, waited for their leader to pass sentence. But he remained silent, his face implacable.

Chapter VII

The sacred hill, it seemed, was impervious to Zhoneyut's grief. Formed by rain-filled ravines and worn by the passage of time, the hill on whose summit stood the prominent tombstone of the Holy One met the old soldier with silence. It did not respond to anything, neither his entreaties nor his complaints. Only the tall black obelisk, impervious to the passage of time, seemed to tell him that he must remain firm, as always, and not lose his will to carry on living.

Zhoneyut made the journey back to the *aul* with a troubled heart. The horse had trouble descending the slope which in the rain had now turned to mud. The stallion's legs splayed out on the sodden clay and, after a while, the horse chose an easier descent, moving off onto a narrow white sandy path next to the beaten track.

From this altitude, the *batyr* observed once again the sea in the distance and the pebbly shoreline. Through squally rain the sea appeared dark, gloomy and weak with age, just as he, Zhoneyut, felt. Giving it a parting glance, the warrior turned round and did not look in that direction again. He could hear only the muffled rhythm of the waves.

Having descended the hill, wet through, Zhoneyut turned his horse in the direction of his *aul*. Riding on a little, the old man could not contain himself and stopped the horse to take another look at the long promontory that led to the grey sea, smoothed by the rain. He tried to make out the burial mound on top of which was the shrine to Holy Temirbaba, but neither tombstone nor obelisk could be seen. All that was visible was water, cold water all around, governing the sea and pouring over the dry land. Along the track, flowing from higher ground, gurgling torrents rushed by, gathering debris from the desert: drowned beetles, spiders, ants. Further on, at a clearing on flat ground, broad, cloudy puddles had formed on the clay wastelands. Everywhere, as far as the eye could see, the grey autumnal water glinted.

The old warrior hung his head, baring it to the rain flowing down from the skies above. He saw that his horse's legs and belly had been spattered by mud. This excursion to the sacred tombstone had been for nothing. The sacred stone had given him no reply, and now he was returning with a heart emptier and heavier than before he had set out on this lonely pilgrimage. Oh, heart! It had become an old, dilapidated prison, like that which housed those unfortunate *mankurti* who had lost their human countenance; and where the Kazakh *Kiuishi* prisoner had been incarcerated for forty days. Now empty and cold, just like Zhoneyut's heart, only a cold

Large herds of wild goats unexpectedly appeared in view of the *aul* and after them filed their young. The wild animals were free to roam, moving to warmer climes in the south as the summer came to an end. They were not chained up or confined like the domestic animals and livestock to this damp, sodden *aul* on the steppe where the dung had been trampled down by the sheep, camels and horses. The days in autumn are short and soon after the midday meal the sun begins to lose its heat and sets quickly, at which time everyone once more makes off to their yurts. Inside, it is hardly cosy: it has become cold during the course of the day and the damp *kizyak* does not want to light in the fire, instead spitting and barely smouldering, while the pungent smoke rises reluctantly to the opening in the roof.

On the bed with its puffed-up cushions, Zhoneyut either sits solemnly or reclines, spending whole days at home alone. To the right of the yurt's entrance hangs a saddle with a saddlecloth. The saddle has already taken on the scent of the smoke. Forty days since Daulet's death, it was rare for someone to come to the large, dark yurt. But the master of the house rarely left it. The sound of voices could not be heard from inside; only the rasps of an old woman coughing, the pounding of a pestle, the whirring of a spindle, or the clattering of crockery. The old woman makes herself busy in her corner but does not dare speak or approach the master of the house.

When the mourning period was over, people at first would come to visit the old man, but he was unwelcoming to guests, aloof in conversation and non-committal in his replies. Everyone soon left him in peace, except for Anadurdy who continued to look in on him daily. He wanted to distract Zhoneyut from his dark thoughts, to draw his grieving relative into conversation, but he lacked the courage to do so. Having sat with him for a while, sighing every now and again and looking sullenly at Zhoneyut once or twice, he would finally get up and leave.

But in the evenings, a young lad, Kurban, Anadurdy's youngest son, took to visiting the yurt. The old men at this time normally sat at the table in complete silence, barely touching their food. The boy would charge in, breaking the oppressive silence, and liven things up. The old man's eyes would light up and his face would soften with the boy's arrival, but he would not chat with the child or put any questions to him. The boy would sit down unceremoniously to the meal between the old man and the old woman and would drink tea with them. Then he would move to the fire and would begin putting the *kizyak* on it. As he did this, he would recount in a ringing voice all the news from the *aul*. Zhoneyut would stare at the fire in silence. It was not clear whether he heard a single word or if he had taken in anything of the boy's tales.

This time, when he had done attending to the fire and his chat was over, the boy began to fidget as if he were waiting for something. He exchanged glances with the old woman, who knew what it was he was after and threw furtive glances at the old man. Then, noticing the old man's indifference to all around him, the boy began to sneak over to the latticed wall of the yurt, where Daulet's *dutar* was hanging in its cover. Stopping in front of the instrument, Kurban looked round once more at old Zhoneyut, but still he was engrossed in his own thoughts. At this the boy, knowing that the worst that could happen was that he would receive a whipping, made up his mind and cautiously stretched out his hand towards the instrument to remove it from the wall. He crouched down and drew the *dutar* from its cover. The boy's eyes gleamed.

Zhoneyut noticed none of this and continued to sit looking at the fire. The dry, brittle brick of cattle dung, *kizyak*, gathered on the steppe during the hot summer by the mute *mankurti*, had faded from being in the sun and started to blaze instantly, giving off a lilac flame. When it was thrown onto the fire, the *kizyak* burned up in no time at all leaving only a handful of grey ash behind. But then the blackened poker, covered in thick soot, began to turn over and rake at the heart of the fire, and another piece of *kizyak* was thrown onto the flattened ambers. This light, dry fuel gave off, once more, a flash of lilac flame in which everything burned quickly leaving almost nothing.

How insatiable is the kingdom of fire, how almighty the merciless flame! It consumes everything and then all that remains are a few grey cinders. Such is the nature of human life – everything is decided by the power of the flame. The large flame devours the small one. The strong devour the weak. Then the strong are devoured by an even stronger force. And so it goes on, endlessly. Everything around us smoulders, glows, burns, is reduced to ashes and turns to dust. So, what purpose is there in all this endless, continual burning of life which cannot be restrained?

When more *kizyak* was thrown on, the fire burned even stronger, the heat warming the face; Zhoneyut felt the cold in his old age, exhausted from the torpor of his existence. Engrossed in his thoughts, the warrior still paid no attention to what was going on around him.

Suddenly, a muffled sound came from behind his back and he turned. Little Kurban quickly let go of the *dutar*, moving his hands away from the instrument as if his fingers had been burned.

'So that's what you're after! Go on, take it and make yourself scarce. You can strum it at home.'

The boy could not believe his ears and was overjoyed. He jumped to his feet and, clutching the *dutar* to his chest, raced out of the yurt. This incident slipped from Zhoneyut's mind immediately. He was more concerned that he had lost his train of thought – he had been mulling over something important when Kurban's strumming had interrupted him. Unable to retrieve his thoughts, Zhoneyut plumped the cushion and stuffed it underneath him.

The old woman removed the cauldron containing boiled meat from the hearth. It had been a long time since they had sat down to a sumptuous feast with many guests in the house, as they had often done in the good old days – and now it was unlikely to happen. Zhoneyut's wife spread a short cloth in front of her husband on which she placed an old wooden bowl, all faded with the edges chipped, and poured some hot soup into it up to the halfway mark. The old man had gone off his food of late. Now all he took from the platter were two pieces of thinly sliced meat which he chewed reluctantly, swallowed, then brought the bowl to his lips and put it down again. Then he moved away.

The old woman cleared the things away, rinsed out the dishes in a tub, and chucked out the slops on the hot ash in the fire where they sizzled. A short while later she blew out the oil lamp which had thick smoke coming from it and the yurt was plunged into darkness.

The old people went to bed earlier than everyone else in the *aul* and woke up later than many. Unable to sleep, they lay in the darkness until the early hours, listening out for any sound. The autumn night seemed to engulf the remote Turkmen *aul*. Only the drops of water in the chimney broke the silence. No other sound was heard; neither dogs barking, nor sheep bleating, nor horses snorting. It was the rain and cold making the nights and days damp and unpleasant. The wild animals hid in their lairs, sleeping in their dens instead of foraging the steppe.

But Zhoneyut does not sleep. He has forgotten what sleep is. Whether he is sitting at home or lying in bed, he is listening out for something in the silence of the yurt. Is he waiting for his enemies to come, trying to detect the approach of their raid while they are still far off? No. He had overheard the elders saying that, at this time, in such inclement weather – thanks be to Allah! – everything had gone quiet. And Zhoneyut himself had also quietened: he no longer thought about raids. It had even been a while since the Mambetpana tribe had sent news of stolen livestock or attacks. Evidently, the *bai*'s wealth and well-fed herds were of no interest to the plunderers just now.

One day, Anadurdy brought news of how he had met an acquaintance, a Kazakh hunter, on the steppe and he had told Anadurdy that Dyiuimkara had moved with his horde from the high ground to the valley where the winter mountain passes ran. Zhoneyut livened up a little on hearing this news: he began to wait impatiently for the Adai plunderers to come. But a month had already passed and the enemy had not appeared, even though it would have been a golden opportunity for them.

Zhoneyut had a dream: it was as if one of his people – he could not recall who – came riding up from the north and, waving his arms, shouted out something unintelligible, something disturbing. But in the dream, Zhoneyut guessed what it was the frightened *dzhigit* was yelling: Dyiuimkara had appeared in the north. At last his ferocious enemy was coming to meet him! The warrior raced to saddle his horse, but the Argamak had disappeared somewhere. 'Heh, you people!' Zhoneyut tried to say. 'Get me a horse!' But he had lost his voice, and only a croaking sound came from his mouth. He found it difficult to breathe, and began waving his arms and groaning pitifully. Then his wife shook him awake.

He opened his eyes and lay still in bed taking in the sounds coming from the roadway. The neighbour could be heard working away furiously with her pestle and mortar, while at the same time shouting out something to her son who was tending a young camel on the edge of the *aul*. The boy answered her from afar in a high, ringing voice.

Since that time, Zhoneyut had stopped waiting for Dyiuimkara to appear. Obviously, it was not fated that they come to blows in a duel which would be the end for one of them. Zhoneyut had heard that Dyiuimkara was famed not only for his fighting skills and for being a great *batyr*, but that he had also become very wealthy, a true *bai*. This meant that he probably had enough troubles right now, since it is no easy thing tending one's riches. And it is not easy in such awful weather to manage countless livestock. Furthermore, the *bai* Dyiuimkara was not going to set off on an incursion in order to avenge some *Kiuishi*, whom the Turkmen had at first held prisoner and then presumably executed. It was clear that no one amongst the Adai was prepared to risk his life for the sake of avenging that wretched *dombra* player.

Old Zhoneyut turned over on his other side. Now that he could no longer sleep he would have to toss and turn in his bed until morning. From the day that he had put to death the prisoner, he had been plagued with insomnia. He had no rest even in a soft bed – it was as if thorns had been placed there. When he used to return from campaigns he would sometimes sleep for several days without waking. This was how a farmer would sleep after finishing his heavy harvest labour in the autumn – even were you to slice off his ears, he would not wake up.

So he had lost his rest and sleep. As soon as his head hit the pillow and he shut his eyes, he would see the low-lying land between the two flat-topped hills, all thickly covered with dark weeds of the *tugai* bush. The old caravan road cuts across this low-lying land, running down from one hill to another. It stretches from Manghistau and then forks off into two paths, one leading to Khiva and the other to Balkhash. Travellers are using this road at all times of the year, moving their goods from one place to another.

There, in the overgrown hollow, forty horsemen rode in file led by Zhoneyut. The Kazakh prisoner was with them. They had got to the place too early, just after midday, and sheltered from the heat in the bushes and, setting an ambush, sat waiting for darkness.

However, not one caravan or traveller went past during that time. After the sun had set, the group emerged from their cover and reached the road. The *dzhigits* dismounted. There was not a soul anywhere. The cover of night had descended over the edge of the sky in the south-west, and blanketed the valley. Neither the road nor the dense undergrowth could be made out in the darkness.

Three of the group took with them spades that had been strapped to the saddles and, turning up the sleeves of their robes, began to dig a hole at the roadside. The diggers were soon replaced by others and then more and, as there were many of them, a deep hole, at least five feet deep, was soon ready. They dragged the prisoner off the horse and, without even removing the fetters, dropped him into the tomb while still alive. The poor soul whined and groaned quietly, gazing around in desperation, but no one paid him heed. Not a word was uttered; everything passed off in total silence. Three men hastily filled in the hole, with the prisoner in it, and the edges were levelled off. Only the prisoner's head remained protruding from the ground. The silence was eerie: not a word had passed the prisoner's lips. Having finished their job, his tormentors jumped back on their horses and cantered off in the direction of the *aul*. The dark head on the ground turned and followed after the riders as they moved off in the darkness. And the prisoner, buried up to his neck, was soon left alone in the wilderness of death.

The riders plunged into the night and lashing their horses, raced along the road overgrown with *tugai* thickets. The ghostly silhouettes of trees flew by; it seemed to the steppe fighters that the valley of death from which they were trying to escape was full of ghouls, ready to fall upon them from behind. The riders whipped their horses harder still, coming off the road and into scrubland, headstrong, pushing through the undergrowth, snapping the saplings and scattering the wild animals – boar, deer and the big cats. Snakes hissed beneath the trampling hooves.

The Turkmen's hurried retreat from the valley, where the horrifying burial had taken place, had passed off without a word spoken. Zhoneyut himself, and each man absorbed in his own thoughts as if they had been riding alone. After any successful raid, hurrying home, they would usually chat among themselves merrily, with chat and laughter ringing across the steppe. But that night, their *papakhas* lowered to the horses' necks and with intensity in their eyes, the *dzhigits* moved as if fleeing an enemy.

The moon rose, and by its hazy light, the black riders emerged from the *tugai* into open country, at length reaching the *aul* before sunrise. Still in silence they parted, off to their homes. The evening before, they had ridden out, noisily whooping, but now they slunk home like thieves.

Later that day, none of them ventured from the yurts. Almost ridden to death, hobbling, and with foamy muzzles, the horses were let out to graze on the meadows behind the *aul*. An eerie silence lay across the *aul* until evening. While the sun was still setting behind a blood-red sky, the yurts' entrances remained shut and folk were preparing for bed. Only the horses beyond the perimetor of the settlement could be heard snorting as they grazed, the young camels tethered by the yurts lay down to sleep.

It was as if the Angel of Death, Azrayil, hovered over the steppe and the deserted-looking *aul*. That night in the yurts no one could sleep. Amid heavy sighs there was tossing and turning. Moonlight crept through the slats and crevices of the yurts in rays like spears. People watched in the silence. Now they seemed apprehensive not only of an armed enemy creeping up on the *aul* but also of some lost, peace-loving soul appearing out of the night. They quaked in their beds even at the neighing of a horse.

Zhoneyut, in his large dark yurt, was not sleeping either. He closed his eyes in exhaustion only to open them up again immediately. All the time he was listening, listening out for something. He endured this until the early hours. A nightjar landed on the pile of *kizyak* which the *mankurt* prisoners had gathered and heaped up by the yurt. It chirped for a long time and then flew off. A minute later, its voice could be heard farther off, from the other side of the *aul*. In the ensuing silence only the subdued sighs of the old woman were audible as she fretted over her husband. A mouse scratched away at the base of the flour bin, trying to grind through it. Suddenly, Zhoneyut the warrior experienced a wave of fear in his own home, in his native *aul*, hidden amongst the hills and steppe, at the very core of the earth. This was the first time in his life that the old soldier had felt such fear. Something strange, awful and irredeemable had occurred: there was no reversing it. The shaft of moonlight moved across the yurt and caught the dagger hanging on the wall. He felt like grabbing hold of it so as to restore his confidence and peace of mind. Somewhere far off, beyond the *aul*, a jackal howled. A fox barked back in reply. They had probably crossed each other at the old animal burial ground and were fighting over some carrion, angrily snapping and baring their teeth at each other.

How interminable is the night! Sleep evaded Zhoneyut and, even by squeezing his eyes tight, he could not rid himself of the persistent vision: the caravan road and above, the moon just as bright, and at the roadside the round head of the buried *kiuishi* still protruding from the ground. The head, with an expression of mild entreaty in its eyes, gazing towards the riders in their *papakhas* who had moved off. The man buried up to his neck is terrified. How unbearable is the pain in his body, his hands and legs bound still in iron fetters! Ants crawl over his face, clamming in a deathly sweat. In his chest, crushed by the heavy clay, his heart beats desperately. The surrounding earth distresses his thumping heartbeat. Now the head of the buried *dombra* player slowly turns in the other direction. What was that he saw? Some large indistinct forms come creeping out of the *tugai*. They move slowly, coming nearer. The man's eyes are filled with horror; he wants to cry out in fear but he does not dare to. He thinks that if he screams, filling the whole moonlit world with his cry, then the monstrous shadows will hop on him and smother him. 'It is better to cower in silent fear. What if these were not monsters but my executioners returned to finish me off or have taken pity and are returning to dig me out?' Listening attentively he thought he could hear a sound of horses' hooves. But no, it was not horses' hooves – it was the sound of the heavy step of Death approaching.

Meanwhile, the black shadows had closed in around him. The head in the ground moved in alarm: the shadows creeping up on him, turned out to be animals – the hairy snouts and bared teeth of jackals, their tongues hanging from their jaws. They had picked up the scent of human flesh. Now they would fall upon his face and tear at it with their fangs. He shut his eyes. Let them strike soon and tear his head to shreds and then, as jackals do, dig him, all his body, out of the earth.

Zhoneyut rose out of bed and moved to the wall where he seized his dagger. Returning to his bed, he placed his weapon beside him on the blanket and began, with trembling fingers, to stroke the sheath, tracing the inlaid and repoussé patterns. He held on tightly to the familiar haft of his old battle friend. The demons vanished as if they had recoiled from him. The old soldier's heart was beating as if ready to jump from his chest. Gradually, the old man calmed down and laid the weapon at his side. It was quiet in the yurt, quiet and eerie. Even the mouse had ceased chewing the wood of the flour bin. The jackal in the distant burial ground had stopped its yelping. Only in the neighbouring yurt, where Daulet had lived and where now, with winter approaching, they had moved the Kazakh *mankurti*, came the sounds of deep snores and moans, and the grinding of teeth.

Yes, old Zhoneyut had gradually calmed down, but one tormenting thought plagued him. It was the thought of what would have happened if he, Zhoneyut, had not executed the *dombra* player and had not buried him alive. What would have happened? The warrior had learned from Anadurdy that it had been the very Kazakh *dombra* player with whom Daulet had competed in the Adai contest. They had shared first prize because the contest judges had considered them equally skilled musicians. And it had happened that he was the very one taken hostage by the troop as it returned with Daulet's body. The warrior's last son was a true *dzhigit*, and what of this *Kiuishi*? This half-starved weakling was no soldier! To avenge Daulet's death a lusty fighter was needed, one who could be cut up into pieces and fed to the dogs!

Yet what would have actually happened if Zhoneyut had spared the Kazakh's life and sent him home safe and sound? What would Zhoneyut's people have said? They would have said that Zhoneyut, their chieftain, had grown old and had become soft out of grief and like a woman; that he was not the same *batyr* who had led them in campaigns and had always triumphed. This is what his people, like all the other Turkmen tribes, would have said. Then the reputation of the great *batyr* would have died, his authority over his people would have come to an end, and he would never have been able to take vengeance on the Adai for the death of his three sons. By ordering the execution of the Kazakh prisoner and burying him alive at the side of the caravan road along which the Kazakhs travel either to Konrat or to Khorezm to buy provisions, he could be sure that the Kazakhs would see this terrible deed and, with blood boiling from rage and indignation, they would rush to wreak vengeance. Dyiuimkara himself would be horrified and outraged. It was the vile Dyiuimkara who had killed his brother Kekbor, and whose tribe had brought so much misfortune on the Turkmen people; who had taken the life of Daulet. Dyiuimkara would be horrifed and outraged and then would surely set out on a campaign of vengeance.

And so Zhoneyut would again go into battle with the Adai and the spirit of his ancestors would help bear him up. He would tear out the throat of his enemy and make him choke on his own blood! Vengeance! Vengeance was what the old *batyr* needed. Only when he had had his revenge could he die in peace, and if he were to die in battle, then so be it – his life was of no more value than those of his three sons. Whatever happened, he would leave his people a fiery legacy, even if only one of his tribesmen were left standing. The *batyr* would never call for a reconciliation or truce, or for mutual forgiveness and submission, like the *Kiuishi* had suggested in his playing before he had him taken away to die. Yet in his very death, that damned *Kiuishi* continued to call for the same thing. He continued to torture the soul of old Zhoneyut with the horror of a nightmare, with his deep-set eyes and his head protruding from the ground as if summoning him to a ritual discussion.

'You, unfortunate *Kiuishi*!' Zhoneyut declared to himself. 'Maybe Allah will not desert you and people will pass by on that road, on their way to Khiva or Konrat, and will see you and dig you out alive. Or else, you will die a terrible death in a deserted place. Well then, *Kiuishi*, accept your fate with dignity. Is your life worth more than that of Klych, or Alpan or my brother, Kekbor? And what about Daulet: is it worth more than his?

'Yes, you did the right thing,' the old warrior said to himself. 'All was as it should be. You did not show the enemy your weakness. You let them know that you are as ruthless with them as you always have been.'

After these reflections, Zhoneyut felt more at ease. His heart stopped racing. He even managed a short sleep. Yet he dreamed again that the Adai *Kiuishi* had overpowered him, and tormented him. All that had been churned up in Zhoneyut's soul by the music, which came rushing back to him. He dreamed again of the valley, overgrown with dark thickets between the two ridges through which ran the caravan road. He was making his way through the dense undergrowth, with small animals scurrying underfoot, snakes hissing; the thorny bushes clinging onto his arms as if they were trying to ensnare him. The path through these bushes was a long and tortuous one. At last he came out of the undergrowth and could see the road ahead, but it became even harder to take a step forward as his legs sank into shifting sands.

Then, from behind him, he thought he heard the clatter of horses' hooves. Zhoneyut ducked into the bushes and hid. He felt someone's eyes staring at him. He had been followed from the moment he left his *aul*, they probably wanted to know why he had come here. Why *had* he come here? To release the prisoner whom he had condemned to death? No, no! That would have made him a laughingstock. They would have said that he was ashamed of what he had done, that the head protruding from the ground terrified him or that he, a veteran warrior, had taken pity on the prisoner.

And there it was, the head protruding from the ground in the flat area by the roadside. No one had seen it: there were not many passers-by at this time of year on the caravan road. Surely Zhoneyut could not free this *Kiuishi* whom he, Zhoneyut, had ordered to be buried alive. His commands must be unmoving. It was not a matter of whether to release the Kazakh or not: the main thing was that he was still alive. The dark head was visible by the light of the moon. Neither animals nor demons had devoured him: he was still in one piece, his face turned the other way, his chin sunk in the sand.

Should he go over to it? But why? How would it be possible, since whoever was secretly following him would see? It would be better to come back at night and by day to hide up in the *tugai*. At night he could go over to the head and sit beside it to guard it and drive away any animals, until someone came along the road and saw it. Then the Kazakhs would free their man and dig him out. Zhoneyut thought that the fellow could hold out for about three days, during which some Kazakhs were bound to pass by. Yes, Zhoneyut would keep watch over this head for three nights. He would tell them in the *aul* that he had been hunting. But now he had the impression that the head had moved and, turning in his direction, had opened its eyes. The desire to go over to it and to sit down and talk was overwhelming. In several hurried paces, Zhoneyut crossed the deserted space between the road and the undergrowth and went up to the head and crouched down.

In his dream it seemed to Zhoneyut that the head, ghostly in the moonlight, was none other than that of his dead son, Daulet! Without even glancing at his father, Daulet's head turned again, to look away. What intense, unearthly sorrow was on the face of his son, entrapped in the earth! What father's heart could endure such a terrible encounter? Oh, Allah! You can be cruel but you are always just. In his dream, Zhoneyut made haste to save his son. He began to scrabble away at the earth around the head, and it was soft, like dust; but he could not hold it in his hands and it kept slipping through his fingers as he was digging. Daulet, as if understanding the futility of his father's efforts, did not turn his head towards him. Letting his hands drop feebly, Zhoneyut ceased digging. At that moment something in the very heart of the old *batyr* finally burst and tore out into the world and Zhoneyut, raising his hands to the sky, let out a primeval scream: 'My dear son! Say something! Why do you not speak?'

Zhoneyut did not recognise his own voice, it was so hoarse. He woke in tears. The faint rays of dawn slanted through the opening in the roof of the yurt. Everything in his home that his eyes lay upon seemed illusory: the felt of the walls, the withies of the frame, and all their belongings a lifeless heap. He could not fathom whether he was dreaming this, or whether life itself had become dream-like. Hoping that to address God might resolve matters, he decided to pray. Wiping away his tears, the old *batyr* whispered a supplication.

Outside the yurt all was quiet except for the protracted bleating of a young camel. The mother camel, ready to give milk, arose, her joints clicking as she straightened out her legs. The old woman was already outside, clattering around with the milk pail.

From that night onwards, Zhoneyut lost sense of what was dream and what reality. The old soul could no longer distinguish between the two and for him life would remain that way until the very end. The days were agonising and dragged interminably. It had seemed only recently that time would pass without his noticing: a month would fly by like a day. But like a fox in a lair the old man shut himself away in his yurt and, lying on his bed, waited and waited. During the night he would long for the sun to rise and morning to appear; during the day he could scarcely endure the tedious hours until evening; he longed for night. Before, he would note the passing of time, the progression of the days, by the significant events that occurred: the campaigns, the raids, the welcoming and seeing-off of honoured guests. They would say; 'Two days after Mambetpana's departure . . .' or 'Three days before the raid on the Adai, when we took the six *mankurti* prisoners . . .' Now he no longer spoke his thoughts aloud, but kept them to himself.

We now know that during these last days of his life, Zhoneyut spent most of his time in a dream-like existence. It was as if all those in the district had forgotten about him; even those who had at one time been his faithful assistants and helpers no longer came to the old *batyr*. The last time that they had been with him was on the night of the Kazakh prisoner's burial. That illustrious band of the forty *dzhigits* who had loyally served their chieftain, carrying out unquestioningly any order of his, had on that fateful day set out with Zhoneyut without demur to the caravan road, dug the hole and buried the prisoner there alive. They had all returned to the *aul* together and had ridden off to their respective homes without a word. From that day on, Zhoneyut had not seen any of them.

'What were they doing now?' wondered Zhoneyut. He imagined them sitting in their yurts, making themselves busy with the fire and fussing round the women and children. Maybe some were repairing their boots while others were softening a hide, or even soldering the holes in the old cauldrons.

Now it was a rare thing for an elder to look in on old Zhoneyut and inform him of the state of the pasture lands, talk of the mowing and the dried-up water holes and other such day-to-day matters. Before, a grey-bearded elder would turn up and sitting in the place of honour reminisce over old times – the illustrious deeds of forebears and the *batyri*, all of them with such unparalleled skill with the spear and sword. Hitherto they would have recounted all this with the aim of pleasing the master of the house, glancing at him gravely and following every movement of his stern face. Now no one mentioned the legendary *batyri*. Instead, they would prattle on about everyday affairs, gossip-mongering, forgetting their status, that they ought to be the bearers of wise words. Zhoneyut realised that the power he once had had gone and that he no longer held sway. They no longer showed him deference or respect. Zhoneyut did not appreciate having visitors, and would sit in front of them with a cold expression in his dark eyes. So it was rare for someone to look in on him, not even his neighbours. The familiar sounds of daily life were the only ones to filter through to the yurt: someone pounding their mortar with a pestle, or tapping with a hammer; the scraping of a ladle at a cauldron, or someone rattling in a loud voice about some kid goat or a camel which had wandered off, or the rustling sounds of the mute *mankurti* shaking the dry slabs of *kizyak* from their sacks.

What was left to talk about with his neighbours? He would smile bitterly and become again immersed in his own thoughts. If only he could speak to that Kazakh *dombra* player. To him alone could Zhoneyut have divulged his sorrow, since it was he who had revealed to Zhoneyut through his music what lay deep in his old heart. But it was not possible to speak to the *dombra* player. It tormented him even to think about such a conversation. He tried to think of something else, or people would guess what was on his mind and think that he, the *batyr* Zhoneyut, had lost his senses.

In his dreams he became more daringly kind-hearted. It was easy for him to express himself freely in his dreams. The trivial routine no longer concerned him. In his dreams he would quietly complain to the *dombra* player of how meaningless life was. The musician would listen attentively to the old *batyr,* and always with a kind smile. 'What do you want me to say?' the *Kiuishi* seemed to say. 'I have already revealed what you wanted to hear in my *kiuiy*. Do you remember?'

'Of course I remember,' replied Zhoneyut without any embarrassment, 'but allow me to contradict you, *Kiuishi*. Yes, it is true that I cried when I heard you play. But that does not mean that I should go back on all that I know. If people are given a licence, if they do not know the meaning of fear, they will lose all discipline and become like mud on the road, making it possible for any scoundrel to order them about. People have to be guided and pushed so that they don't backslide.' The gaunt face of the *Kiuishi* only smiled in reply, keeping his silence. He looked into the distance and then, in a quiet voice, said, as if talking about himself: 'An impatient *batyr* can be drawn forward by the slightest whim, but a patient one only by a lofty dream.'

Zhoncyut awoke from these exhausting conversations in a torment. But as soon as he opened his eyes, these wayward thoughts – the passion, the anger and the bitter doubts vanished at once, leaving only unbearable solitude. He had no one to talk to, to share this immense, infinite solitude. The only person who would have understood was the one he had had condemned to a terrible death, the one he had buried alive in the ground. It was only now that the old *batyr* realised that most of all he wanted to show mercy to the *Kiuishi* by releasing him. But he had not done this for fear of being seen as weak by his people; as having lost his courage, strength and the fighting spirit of a chieftain. He had feared the judgement of this contemptible throng and had sacrificed this poor innocent man.

Old Zhoneyut could never forgive himself for this.

He had yet another dream. He was coming out of the undergrowth and reached the roadside when he saw something that filled him with horror: a huge grey wolf baring its teeth, and with a hollow growl about to pounce upon the head protruding from the ground. Zhoneyut pulled his gun from its holster and aimed at the beast. But the head gave out an awful scream: 'Don't shoot it! Let me die! Or, even better, kill me yourself!' The wolf turned to look at Zhoneyut and moved away, scuttling off into the bushes. When Zhoneyut, shaking all over, went over to the *Kiuishi's* head, he saw that it had a detached, frowning expression. The old man bent over it and in a guilty voice began to explain that he had killed him in order to entice Dyuimkara into a reprisal. But that damned Dyuimkara had not even raised a finger to avenge the death of his fellow tribesman.

The warrior Zhoneyut was striving to justify himself but it was as if the condemned man had turned his at first, then moving closer. He opened his eyes, listening out for the sounds, and saw that he was on the steppe. All around him was the desert with not a soul to be seen. The music seemed to be coming from under the ground. Oh, what warm, familiar music. This was unbearable for Zhoneyut! He turned around and fled with all the strength he could muster. But it was impossible to escape the melody of the *kiuiy* and the sound of the *dombra*. The music flew in pursuit of him, enveloping his soul and extinguishing it.

Old Zhoneyut threw off the blanket and leaped from his bed. Barefoot, and dressed only in his white undergarments, he dashed towards the exit of the yurt, sticking his fingers in his ears as he ran. He was shouting out unintelligibly in a thin voice, like that of a child. While running, he banged his head on the lintel and, reeling like a soldier receiving an arrow in his heart, collapsed with a deep groan face downwards on the threshold.

That morning, noticing that her husband had dozed off, the old woman had picked up her loom and gone in search of her neighbours, to Anadurdy's yurt where the boy, Kurban, sat strumming the *dutar*. Of late, Kurban had become inseparable from the instrument which had been passed on to him so unexpectedly. This morning he had thought of the *kiuiy* which the prisoner *dombra* player from the Adai tribe had played on the last day of his life, and had begun to pluck out the tune. Kurban had been standing outside the yurt with his ear pressed to the felt wall when the musician had started playing. Now he could recall clearly the first sounds of the introduction which resembled the ebullience of a fast-flowing river, soon turning into the swift, measured gallop of a steppe horse. Kurban played the music confidently, while old Anadurdy sat opposite him listening with his head lowered. It was then that the final heavy groans of the dying Zhoneyut reached the yurt. They rushed over and saw the old *batyr* lying on his threshold, bent double, as if a flying arrow had pierced his heart. When they turned the body over, Zhoneyut's soul had left its shrunken body, and soared into the sky.

Kesushka – diminutive mixed (Kazakh-Russian) term for a traditional Kazakh tea bowl.

Kiuishi – musician.

Kiuiy – musical composition for the dombra.

Kizyak – fuel made of cattle dung.

Koshma – traditional Kazakh felt, felt cloth.

Kumgan – traditional Kazakh jar (*plural*, kumgani).

Mankurt (*plural*, mankurti) – the victim of a torture whereby the hair is shaved off and a thin piece of leather fitted over the skull. There is a transferred meaning (especially in contemporary Kazakh) – a déraciné who wants nothing to do with his native culture, language and traditions.

Papakha – sheepskin hat, traditional in the Caucasus.

Saksaul – (*Haloxylon*), a plant with a hard stem and roots, usually used as fuel to cook food.

Sarbaz – warrior (*plural*, sarbazi).

Shaitan – devil or evil spirit.

Siunshi – gift given to the bearer of good news.

Soyil – a club or heavy stick used for fighting (*plural*, soyili).

Tor – an honoured place in a house (usually the side of the table facing towards the door).

Tugai – type of bush.

Yashmak – veil, worn by women, covering the head and face.

Yurt – traditional dwelling of nomads, clad in felt or skins on a lattice frame.

Zhungari – a nation originating from western China, invaders of Kazakh territory. Zhungars (or Dzungars) were defeated by Kazakhs with Russian imperial help in the 18th century.

Zindan – prison.